A MAYFAIR CHRISTMAS CAROL

A Marcia Banks and Buddy Mystery

Kassandra Lamb

Published by ***misterio press LLC***

Cover art by Melinda VanLone, Book Cover Corner

Photo credit: silhouette of woman and dog by Majivecka (right to use purchased through Dreamstime.com)

ISBN: 978-1-947287-02-0

CHAPTER ONE

This is crazy!

Yeah, it had been my idea to begin with. But it was still crazy.

I'd suggested we call a meeting to discuss ways we could promote our small Florida town of Mayfair as a tourist destination. The first few people I'd approached seemed skeptical, but the tide turned when I'd gotten the two matriarchs of the town invested in the idea.

Now one of those matriarchs—the saner of the two, I had thought—was right in the middle of the craziness. And the other, the one who normally thrived on crazy ideas, was alternating between staring at the toes of her moccasins and plucking lint from her old brown sweater. The sweater and the footwear were Edna Mayfair's only concessions to the cool evening. Otherwise, she was attired in one of her usual brightly colored and shapeless muumuus.

Even Edna's black and white Springer Spaniels, Bennie and Bo, were subdued, lying quietly at her feet instead of pestering the people around them for head pats and ear scratches.

My own four-legged companion, Buddy, a Black Lab and Rottie

mix, sat beside my chair. My favorite two-legged companion, Will Haines, had the good sense to stay home.

Where I now fervently wished I was. Unfortunately, the prominent position of my seat—aisle end of the second row of the Methodist church's parish hall—and the fact that the woman leading the meeting had ridden to the church with me kept me from trying to unobtrusively slip out.

The noise level in the large room rose a couple of decibels. Warm bodies and heated discussions made the air stuffy. I lifted the weight of my auburn hair off of my neck for a moment.

Buddy rested his black chin on my knee and gave me a soulful look. I suspected he wanted to whine but was too well-behaved to do so. Surely the noise was hurting his ears.

I was trying to decide how to rein in the chaos when a sharp series of cracks split the air.

We all jumped and the competing conversations died away. Heads turned toward the front of the room, where Sherie Wells had improvised a gavel with a large metal spoon.

She smacked it against the wooden table in front of her one more time and silence reigned.

"Before we go any further," she said in a loud, schoolmarm voice, "we should vote."

Nods and affirmative rumbles around me.

"All those in favor of establishing the Mayfair Chamber of Commerce, raise your hand." She raised her own hand and made a come-on gesture with the other. Her silky cream-colored blouse sleeve fell away from her wrist, revealing a clump of gold bracelets sparkling against her mahogany-brown skin.

Despite having been retired for as long as I'd known her, Sherie did not let her appearance slide, not even for a minute. Since she lived next door to me, I'd caught glimpses of her in her mint green terrycloth robe on occasion. She looked regal even in that attire.

Every hand in the place was raised, best I could tell, including Edna's.

Sherie nodded briskly, the smooth, still mostly black chignon on the back of her head bobbing. "Good." She glanced at the other woman seated at the table.

Charlene Woodward, blonde, fortyish, and built like a stick, had apparently been assigned a new role, recording secretary of the about-to-be-minted Chamber of Commerce. She was already Mayfair's part-time postmistress, our sole mail carrier, and during the months of our prolonged summer—from mid-April through October—she and her husband ran a snow cone stand in one corner of the church parking lot. The snow cones probably had more to do with high Sunday school attendance than the curriculum did.

Charlene mumbled, "Chamber of Commerce unanimously passed," as she scribbled on the yellow lined pad in front of her.

"Now," Sherie said, "who is in favor of holding a Christmas event?"

Hands waved in the air again, Edna Mayfair's conspicuously missing. But her great nephew Dexter, sitting beside her, was waving his arm back and forth as if asking permission to go to the restroom. A big grin split his boyish face, attached to a man's body.

Sherie gave him a small smile, then glanced at Edna with worry in her eyes. Nonetheless, she forged ahead. "How many in favor of a Victorian theme?"

Fewer hands this time, although still clearly a majority, and pandemonium erupted again.

I tuned out at that point. Later I would wish I hadn't.

It was almost ten by the time the meeting adjourned. I was glad about two things. One, that everyone seemed enthusiastic about the idea of improving our town's economic status by attempting to attract tourists. And two, that Sherie had taken the lead.

I'd hoped that she and/or Edna would do so. Even though the Chamber of Commerce had been my idea, I was enough of a newcomer—having lived in Mayfair for just under three years—that I felt weird taking on a leadership role.

Edna had been gung-ho until the Christmas festivities discussion had taken over the agenda. Then she'd let Sherie take the lead.

Was the octogenarian a closet Scrooge?

She always decorated the Mayfair Motel for Christmas, with fake garlands of greens and holly berries wrapped around anything upright and skinny that didn't move. But I wasn't real sure to what degree she actually celebrated the holiday, because I usually left around December twentieth to drive north to visit my family in Maryland.

Now that I thought about it, whenever I'd asked how her holidays had been, she usually answered with words like *peaceful* and *relaxing* and then changed the subject.

As I drove us home, Sherie was quiet, staring out her side window. Nearing the town's only street light—Edna paid for the electricity to light it—she sat up straighter.

Ahead were Dexter and Edna, walking up the sidewalk to the wide verandah that adorned the front of the new motel, erected on the site of the old one that had been burned down by a crazy person the previous spring.

I tapped my horn and they both turned and waved. We waved back, although I doubted they could see us inside the dark car. Then I rounded the curve and pointed us toward our cottages at the end of a longish stretch of road with no development on either side. At least no recent development. The skeletons of several old shacks to our left were slowly being consumed by termites and the rampant foliage of tropical plants.

During the heyday of Mayfair in the 1960s, the black maintenance staff of the Mayfair Alligator Farm had lived along this stretch, segregated from the white residents of the town. Sherie's father-in-law had been the maintenance supervisor.

"Wish I knew what got into Edna tonight," Sherie suddenly piped up, as I pulled to the curb in front of our houses.

"Me too. I suggested the Chamber of Commerce idea as a way to make her motel more successful, so she could hire some staff and not work so hard."

Sherie turned her head and studied me. Her porch light shone on her face. "Edna doesn't know how to *not* work so hard. Her brother was like that too. One time, Mr. Mayfair decided to expand the alligator farm. Daddy Wells got the men workin' on clearin' the land, my daddy among 'em." Her Southern accent thickened as she waxed nostalgic.

"Jason and I were in high school then. We'd just started datin'..." She paused, a slight smile on her lips. Jason Wells had been the love of her life, her only love—high school sweetheart and later husband of twenty-some years, sadly now deceased for at least ten. "They had plenty of workers then to do the work. The gator farm was still doin' well. But Mr. Mayfair, he wasn't the type to stand by and watch others labor. He rolled up his sleeves, literally, and worked right along side of 'em."

She pointed off to her right, away from the houses. "That area right there across from us, behind the old shacks, where they're goin' to build the skating rink."

"Wha'? A skating rink!" I shook my head, sure I had misheard her. "As in ice skating? In Florida?" My voice ended on a bit of a squeak.

She turned back to me. "Yes, ice skating, with some kind of freon tubes underneath the ice to keep it frozen." She shook her finger in mock outrage. "I thought you looked a little glazed over, toward the end of things this evening. You weren't paying attention, were you?

They voted to build the rink as part of our winter extravaganza. And some of the ladies are making Victorian costumes for the skaters to wear."

I hoped the inside of the car was dark enough that Sherie couldn't tell I was rolling my eyes.

The rumble of machinery woke me for the third morning in a row. As I pulled my pillow up over my head, I once again wondered at the connections either Sherie or Edna must have with the county development office in order to score a building permit so quickly.

Yes, Edna had climbed aboard the insanity train once several folks had pointed out how lucrative the whole venture could be. After all, crazy money-making schemes were the lifeblood of the Mayfair clan.

Awhile later, I was awakened again, this time by the *lack* of machinery noises. My enjoyment of the peaceful silence was short-lived.

A fist pounding on wood, followed by a frantic voice—male, I think, although I couldn't be sure since it shrilled with desperation. I made out only "*Señora* Wells," followed by several incoherent screeches.

I climbed out of bed and pulled on yesterday's shirt and jeans, then went to the kitchen to make coffee. One might wonder why I wasn't more curious or anxious, but the reality is that few things go as planned in Mayfair—alligators come calling, crazies burn down motels, and termites manage to invade cement-block houses.

Once the coffee was brewing, I headed for the front door to find out what all the ruckus was about.

My blasé attitude evaporated when I stepped out on my front porch and turned to where Sherie Wells was standing on her own porch twenty feet away. Her eyes were wide and her brown skin had a grayish tinge to it. "Where's Will?" she demanded.

"Home, I guess," I stammered. "He's been working a big case, long hours."

"Get him!" Sherie drew the belt of her pale green terrycloth robe snug and, still wearing her bedroom slippers, marched off toward the lot across the street.

My chin dropped at the sight—she normally wouldn't go as far as her mailbox in robe and slippers—but I quickly recovered enough to call after her, "What's going on?"

Without looking back, she yelled, "They've found bones, and a skull."

CHAPTER TWO

I hadn't had to lie to Sherie, thank heavens, since last night was one of the rare occasions when Will actually did sleep in his own bed. More often than not, he was in mine. After all, it's not like we're blushing virgins. We've both been married and divorced.

Will would love to make an honest woman of me. I'm the resistant one, for several reasons, the greatest of which is the lying, two-timing concert pianist back in Baltimore who used to be my husband. So to appease my need to go slow, Will bought the fixer-upper cottage next to mine as an interim step to living together.

Todd had often used the excuse of not wanting to disturb me when he slept in the downstairs TV/guest room on nights he had late rehearsals. It had taken an anonymous phone call for me to catch on that he and one of the symphony's cello players had been rehearsing something other than music during those late nights. And that Todd's reason for sleeping elsewhere was so I wouldn't smell another woman's perfume on him.

Thus, when Will didn't answer my knock, a tiny seed of mistrust —which he did not deserve—had me tiptoeing through his house after letting myself in with my key. He had to have come home at some point last night. His unmarked sedan was parked out front.

But what if he isn't alone?

I knew the thought was stupid, but I couldn't help myself. I eased open his slightly ajar bedroom door and froze.

Crapola!

He was standing beside his bed in nothing but his boxers, pointing a Glock at my chest.

"Mar-see-a," he emphasized each syllable of my name, "sneaking into the house of a law enforcement officer is a really bad idea." Under his grumpy tone, his voice sounded as tired as he looked. Normally rugged cheeks were sagging, and his baby blues were bloodshot.

He sat down on the side of the bed and dropped the gun on the covers beside him.

"But you knew it was me," I said.

"I suspected it was, but I couldn't be sure. I'm dealing with some nasty dudes with this case."

"Um, I wouldn't have bothered you this early, but…"

Banging from the front of his house. A loud voice. This time I could make out the words, and the Spanish accent. "*Señor* Haines. *Señora* Wells, she say tell you come quick."

"What the devil?" Will said.

"That's Jorge. He's the foreman of the crew the Chamber of Commerce hired to build the skating rink."

A hard shake of his head. "Run that by me again."

"Remember I told you that we were going to form a Chamber of Commerce for Mayfair? Well, they decided to build an ice skating rink to use during their Christmas extravaganza."

"In Florida?" His voice rose a couple of octaves.

"Yeah, well, that wasn't my idea. I just wanted us to promote the town more as a tourist destination."

Will stood and grabbed a crumpled pair of khaki slacks from the floor. "So now they're having some kind of Christmas thing?" he said as he pulled them on.

"Yeah." I extracted a chambray shirt from his closet and handed it to him. "But there's been a new development."

Renewed banging on Will's front door. "*¡Señor, por favor!*" Jorge sounded like he might burst into tears at any moment.

Will pushed an arm into one shirt sleeve. "This new development seems to have your foreman a little worked up."

"Yeah, they seem to have found a skeleton."

"Marcia, get back behind the tape."

I'd slipped up behind Will, twisting to the side to see past his broad shoulders. "I only wanted to see if I knew him."

"Unlikely. He's been in the ground at least a decade."

"Any ID on him?"

"Marcia, get back!" Somehow Will managed to sound authoritative and long-suffering at the same time.

I retreated to the yellow crime scene tape he'd strung around the perimeter of palmettos, shrubs and saplings that Jorge's backhoe driver hadn't yet uprooted. But I didn't duck under the tape.

It was a small and senseless act of rebellion. I just couldn't bring myself to physically step completely out of the investigation.

I had started this, suggested the Chamber of Commerce idea, the attracting tourists concept. I somehow felt responsible for this latest calamity to befall my adopted town. Instead of becoming a wintertime getaway for Northerners, we'd be that notorious town with buried skeletons, literally.

A van pulled to the side of the road fifty feet away. A blue seal on its side read *District 5 Medical Examiner*. I was both horrified and relieved—at least it wasn't the press.

Will stomped off in that direction, his cell phone plastered to his ear.

I stood frozen. Part of me wanted to inch forward again and see if I could catch a glimpse of the skeleton. Another part wanted to run back to my house, to my dogs, and pretend that the day hadn't begun with Jorge pounding on Sherie Wells's door.

My dogs! They were still in their crates, with the exception of Buddy. I'd left him standing just inside my own front door, his head cocked in his patented what's-up look.

I ducked under the tape and hurried back to my house to let the animals out back before their bladders burst.

When I got back to the lot, two Marion County Sheriff's Department cruisers had arrived, disgorging four uniformed deputies who had taken up positions around the perimeter to discourage the clumps of townspeople from infringing on the crime scene.

Of course, there really wasn't much of a crime scene to process. The field had lain fallow for decades. And it had now been torn up by the backhoe brought in to remove Mother Nature's attempts to reclaim the property.

Will spotted me and came over. "Not much happening now. We have to wait for a forensic anthropologist. He's on his way from Gainesville."

"Like in the TV show, *Bones*?"

He nodded. "There's one who's a visiting professor at the University of Florida."

"Awesome," I said. "Any hints at all from the skeleton as to who he or she may be?"

Will shook his head. "A few scraps of cloth but nothing big enough to tell us anything. We don't even know if it's male or female.

But I'm guessing male, based on the pelvic bone." He paused. "I've been assigned the case."

"But what about the drug case you've been working?"

He glanced down, kicked a clump of dirt. "I'd kinda reached a dead end. Sheriff gave it to two other guys."

Read between the lines—the newbie hadn't produced so yank the rug out from under him. I couldn't help but wonder if Will was running into some prejudice because he was a Northern transplant, a former detective in the Albany, New York Police Department.

"Maybe they figure you've got an edge, living in Mayfair," I said, trying for a positive spin.

He grimaced, then shrugged. "If I'd lived here for any length of time, the sheriff would probably see that as a disadvantage."

Insight jolted through me. Will had to be feeling like a stranger in a strange land. He'd come to Florida four years ago, to take the position of sheriff in a small rural county. He didn't have a lot of friends *per se* in Collins County, but he'd become a part of that community, and his position garnered him a certain level of respect.

Now he was a newly-hired detective in a much larger county, just a cog in a rather big wheel.

I reached out and squeezed his arm. "You know the town loves having their own resident cop."

He grimaced again. "Yeah, well they might not love me so much when I start asking some tough questions."

The forensic anthropologist arrived an hour later. A uniformed deputy came to fetch Will, who was drinking coffee in my kitchen.

I, of course, hustled after them as they crossed the street.

I'd been expecting a beautiful female geek *ala* Temperance Brennan or a stuffy old man. Instead he was a stuffy young man, barely out of graduate school by the looks of him, and wearing a crew-neck sweater that was way too heavy for Florida's mild November weather.

"Dr. Oliver J. Tolliver," he said, sticking out his hand after Will identified himself.

I stifled a snicker. I thought I'd had it bad in school, with kids making fun of the unusual pronunciation of my name—Mar-see-a rather than Marsha. No doubt Oliver Tolliver had encountered even more malicious monsters growing up.

What was his mother thinking?

But the doc, despite his youthful appearance, seemed to know what he was doing. He made measurements and took soil samples and photos from multiple angles, before he would allow any of the bones to be moved. Then he carefully sifted the dirt in the sandy grave, making sure no fragments or other clues had been neglected.

"I'll get back to you as fast as I can," he told Will.

Dr. Tolliver was as good as his word. The preliminary report arrived by fax in thirty-six hours. It confirmed Will's hunch that the skeleton was male.

He was also Caucasian, and the report gave a tentative age of twenty-five to thirty-five. Death had most likely been caused by a blow to the back of the head with a sharp metal object that had almost penetrated the skull. It had left a smooth dent two inches long, a sixteenth of an inch wide, and a quarter of an inch deep. The brain tissue had decayed, but Dr. Tolliver believed the blow had caused a "contrecoup contusion" severe enough to cause death.

In other words, the guy's brain had bounced off the other side of his skull hard enough to kill him.

The bones had been in the ground approximately thirty years. A closer estimate, and better aging, would require some rather expensive tests. Will had told the young doctor to hold off on that.

In the meantime, Will had interviewed everyone in town who had lived here thirty years ago. It hadn't taken long, since that list held only a half dozen names, and some of them were children at the time.

Two were farmers who said that Mr. Mayfair tried his hand at being a gentleman farmer once his alligator farm went belly up. He'd hired itinerant workers at times. Maybe this guy was one of them.

Sherie Wells was on Will's list, but it turned out she and her husband were living and working in Jacksonville at that time. "We came home for holidays, and kept in touch, of course. But I don't recall any talk about someone getting hurt or killed around then."

Edna Mayfair, who should have been Will's best informant as she was the sister of the town's patriarch, was a bit vague about that era. She confirmed that her brother was farming then and he sometimes hired workers from outside the area. But other than that, Will reported, her memory seemed sketchy.

"Have you seen any signs that she's starting to lose it?" Will asked me that evening, as we were finishing up our dinner.

"No, she's normally sharp as a tack." I winced a little inside. My tendency to use old-fashioned sayings, originally picked up from my mother, was being reinforced by hanging out so much with women old enough to *be* my mother.

"Well, she wasn't about this," Will said. "She kept saying she couldn't remember exactly. Maybe it's just because it was so long ago."

"I doubt that's the reason, based on what I was taught about memory in grad school." I have a masters degree in counseling psychology, which so far has been close to worthless, but occasionally I can haul out some useful tidbit of information. "Old people can usually remember things from the distant past better than more recent events. Those old memories are more thoroughly embedded. It's called crystallized intelligence."

Will nodded slightly, appropriately impressed.

"Maybe," I said carefully, "she'd be more forthcoming if I talk to her."

His expression quickly shifted, the slight smile pinching into a grim line, the approval in his eyes morphing to annoyance.

"Come on. How can it hurt?" I asked.

Before he could answer, my phone rang. Caller ID said it was my best friend Becky.

"Hey Beck, you'll never believe what's been going on around here."

Will shook his head rather vehemently.

"What?" I mouthed to him.

"Don't tell her about the bones," he whispered.

"So are you going to tell me," Becky said in my ear, "or leave me hanging?"

"Um…" my mind scrambled for substitute news. "Uh, this crazy town voted to build an ice-skating rink."

"Say wha'? In Florida?"

"Yeah, that's been pretty much everyone's reaction."

When I'd managed to extract myself from the phone conversation with Becky, I said to Will, "Why couldn't I tell her about the skeleton?"

"It's likely the killer is long gone." He pushed his empty plate away. "But in case he's still in the area, I don't want the word getting out that the corpse has been found. Better chance of catching him if he thinks he got away with it."

That all made sense. The local grapevine had long since spread the news all over Mayfair, but the lack of media vehicles and over-dressed reporters sticking microphones in people's faces said that the rest of the world was oblivious to our resident skeleton, so far at least.

Best all around if it stayed that way.

Still, I felt uncomfortable keeping things from Becky. And she knew how to be discreet. She was a massage therapist, and some of her clients were the rich and famous who had residences scattered around the horse country surrounding Ocala.

Then again, she probably would tell her husband, Andy Matthews, who'd replaced Will as sheriff of Collins County. And he might tell some other law enforcement person…

My mind jumped back to Will's words. "Or she?" I said out loud.

"Huh?"

"You used *he* for the killer. It might have been a woman."

"I doubt it." Will touched the back of the crown of his head. "The blow hit him here and he was about my height. I doubt a woman would be tall enough or strong enough to strike such a blow."

"Really?" I got up and grabbed a broom from one corner of the kitchen. Raising it above my head, I playacted bringing it down on Will's where he sat at the table. "Easy peasy if he was sitting down."

Will stood and turned his back to me. "How about now?"

I turned the broom and gently tapped the edge of its bristles against his hair. "If she were at least of average height like me, still quite possible, with enough adrenaline in her system."

He turned, grinning, and mock-wrestled the broom away from me. Then holding me in his arms, he whispered, "Thanks for your input, Little Miss Detective."

I would've taken umbrage at the "Little Miss"—and he knew that, he was trying to rile me up—but I was too busy melting against him as he nuzzled my neck.

Vague was the term Will had used to describe Edna's memories of events in Mayfair thirty years ago. But after a few minutes of talking to her, the word *evasive* kept popping up in my mind.

I'd made a point of taking Buddy out for an early walk, before starting my morning sessions with the two dogs I was currently training. As I'd hoped, I encountered Edna and her pups on the sidewalk by the motel.

Bennie and Bo were nearing three years old, but I thought of them as puppies. Since Edna's idea of discipline was to fuss at them in a fond voice, they still acted like they were six months old. I let Buddy off his leash, since it would just get tangled up with theirs anyway. The three of them chased each other around the motel's parking lot, blurs of white and black.

Edna smiled indulgently at the dogs. This morning, she was wearing black stretch pants with a long-sleeved, man-tailored purple shirt hanging loose around her ample middle—her concession to the reality that guests at a fancy new motel might be put off by an old woman in a muumuu behind the counter. She'd even made an attempt to tame her gray hair, with limited results. It still stuck up in clumps, but there were fewer of them.

The morning air temperature had barely made it into the sixties, but she wore black flip-flops on her swollen feet. There was a limit to how far she was willing to go to look civilized.

"So what do you think about this skeleton they found?" was my opening salvo.

"Not much," Edna said, still watching the dogs. "Probably some Mexican that John hired to pick crops, got in a fight over a woman or somethin'."

"The anthropologist the M.E.'s office sent over says he was probably white."

Edna snorted. "That whippersnapper didn't look old enough to be separated from his mama."

Resisting the urge to agree with her, I decided to throw caution to the wind. Edna tended to prefer blunt to "pussy-footin'," as she called it. "Do you remember anything in particular happening around here about thirty years ago? Any guys competing for the same woman maybe?" After all, she'd brought that up.

Edna shook her head. "Naw, John was tryin' his hand at farmin', and I was busy raisin' Dexter. Not much else goin' on."

"How many people lived here then?"

She shrugged. "Town was startin' to thin out. The young people, in particular, were goin' off to school and not comin' back. Like Sherie and Jason."

She finally turned and looked at me. "Dang, it's good to have her back."

"Edna, she's been back for ten years."

She broke eye contact and ducked her head. "Oh, yeah."

Then she met my gaze again, and her eyes now had a glazed, faraway look in them. "Hey, did I ever tell ya 'bout the time John wrestled a ten-foot bull gator on a bet?"

Don't quit your day job, Edna. You're a lousy actor.

CHAPTER THREE

Buddy and I had rounded the corner onto Mayfair Avenue when I spotted Dexter moving in our direction. His head was down and he was shuffling along, hands in the pockets of his jeans. A faded blue plaid shirt hung open over his white tee shirt.

He jumped a bit when I called his name, then waved. "Hey, Marcia."

"Hey, what's up?" I said as I got closer to him.

His medium-length brown hair was tousled, as if he hadn't bothered to comb it this morning. But his hazel eyes were clear when he made eye contact. "Nothin' much. Just walkin'. Had some thinkin' to do."

We'd converged on the sidewalk not far from the town's improvised ball park, a vacant field where the kids played various sports, mostly baseball. Early on a November weekday morning, the field was deserted.

Some industrious parent had installed two benches, wood planks balanced on cement-block posts. I gestured toward the nearest one. "What were you thinking about?"

He silently accepted the invitation to sit. "That skeleton."

I dropped onto the bench beside him and signaled for Buddy to lie down. He did so and placed his chin on my foot. "What about the skeleton? You have any ideas about who it might be?"

Dexter looked down and scuffed a sneakered foot across the dirt under the bench. "Aunt Edna says it's some transit worker that Grandpa hired."

It took me a beat to realize what he meant. Dexter was taking classes at the community college in Ocala, studying a trade. Welding, I think Edna had said it was. But he also had to pass some general education courses to graduate. He wasn't the brightest bulb on the Christmas tree and he was now taking his second stab at English Composition 101. One of the professor's assignments was to expand one's vocabulary by five words a week.

Apparently *transient* was one of this week's words.

"Who do you think it is?" I asked in a soft voice, sensing from his slouched body language that something was troubling him.

"Oh, I think she's probably right, but how'd he get hit on the head hard enough to kill him? And who buried him?" He glanced quickly at me, then looked down again. "Will's investigatin' it as a murder, ain't he?"

"Yes." I resisted the urge to say more.

"My daddy disappeared a little over thirty years ago."

"You think it's him?"

He shook his head. "No, but I can't help wonderin' if he was the one who kilt some guy and then ran off."

He finally lifted his eyes to meet mine. They were red-rimmed. "It would explain why he just up and left me and Mama."

My chest ached. "How old were you when he left?"

"Four."

"What year was that?"

He stared into space for a couple of seconds, his lips moving slightly. "1983."

I jolted a little, then quickly wiped the surprise from my face. I'd always assumed he was no older than me, early thirties, and maybe even younger than that. He had a round, smooth face and a cheerful, innocent air that made him seem like a perpetual boy.

But he was telling me he was thirty-eight, and if he was right and that skeleton had something to do with his father's disappearance, it had been in the ground thirty-four years.

"Do you remember your father at all?"

He shrugged. "He was big. Used to throw me up in the air and catch me with his big hands. He had funny black marks on his hands." He rubbed his own knuckles. "I'd get all worked up and wet my pants. Then Mama would be annoyed."

"Did they fight much?" I already suspected that they did, from the things Edna had said here and there, calling her former nephew-in-law no good or saying he had a bad temper.

Dexter nodded. "I remember a lot of yellin', and then Mama cryin'. Sometimes she'd have blood on her lip or a black eye. I didn't really understand what that meant back then." He dropped his gaze to the ground and scuffed dirt again. "I asked Aunt Edna 'bout it once, when I was six. She said my daddy beat my mama, but I wasn't to talk 'bout it, especially in front of Grandpa, 'cause it still upset him."

My chest squeezed even tighter but I forced words past the lump in my throat. "When did your mom die?"

"That year, when I was six," he said without looking up. "She was in the hospital for a long time, and that Christmas I asked if she was comin' home for the holiday. She'd been home for my birthday a few months before that. Grandpa's eyes got all watery and he walked out of the room. That's when Aunt Edna told me that Mama had gone to be with the angels for Christmas, and she couldn't come to visit no more…" His voice hitched a little. "'Cause once ya go to heaven, ya can't come back again."

I dug my fingernails into my palms, fighting tears. No wonder Edna was a bit of a Scrooge. Who could blame her if the death of her niece so close to the holidays had soured her on future Christmases?

When I thought I could trust my voice, I asked, "What was wrong with your mom?"

He stared at the ground for a couple of seconds, then finally raised his head. "Ya know, I never did find that out. Aunt Edna just said she was real sick and weren't never gonna get better, and then she was gone."

Fortunately I caught my next thought before it made it to my lips. *Don't you think you have a right to know?*

I also resisted the urge to ask more questions about his mother. I'd already picked at those scabs enough for one day.

But another question occurred to me. "What did your dad do, you know, for a living?"

"Ya know, I don't rightly know that either. I seem to remember he was home most of the time. Maybe he helped out with the gator farm."

That would have been around the time the farm's profits were shrinking, as more and more folks were flocking to the much bigger tourist trap that Walt Disney had built in nearby Orlando.

Dexter had fallen silent, staring at the ground again.

I patted his knee. "You can always talk to me, whenever you need a sounding board."

His face morphed to confusion. "A what?"

"Somebody to bounce things off of, you know, to listen and maybe help you sort stuff out."

"Oh. Thanks, Marcia." He patted my jeans-clad knee, a bit awkwardly. "Yer a good friend."

My throat closed and my eyes stung again. "Thanks, Dexter," I managed to choke out.

As I pushed up off the bench, he caught my arm. I turned and stared down into eyes that were now a cloudy brown more than blue-green.

"If my daddy was a murderer," he said in a low, anguished voice, "does that mean I might have that in me?"

I patted his hand. "Dexter, from what I've seen of your personality, I'd say your mother was a very sweet person, and that you totally take after her."

His eyes cleared but remained confused for a beat. Then his whole face brightened. "Thanks, Marcia."

"You're welcome." I smiled down at him. "Take care."

Over breakfast, I told Will what Edna and Dexter had said, leaving out some of the stuff about his mom that felt like a confidence I shouldn't share. Besides, I didn't want to start bawling in my cereal.

"Hmmph," Will said around a mouthful of Cheerios, "maybe I should ask the sheriff for funds to get the bones dated."

"You think the anthropologist could get any DNA off the skeleton?"

Will shrugged. "I'll ask the doc, but the sheriff may not be willing to spring for DNA testing." He gobbled down another bite of cereal.

"Why not, if he wants you to solve the case?"

He shrugged again. "It's a long shot at best that we'll ever find out what happened. It was three decades ago."

Well you won't for sure, if the stingy sheriff won't pay for anything, my snarky self griped inside my head. I'd been trying harder to keep her restrained lately. Mostly I'd succeeded, but she did pop up now and then. At least I managed not to say her thoughts out loud, most of the time.

"Hmm," I said, "maybe I'll talk to Sherie."

Will had lifted his bowl to his mouth to drink the last of the milk. He froze and looked at me over the rim. "Leave it alone. It's an active case."

Heat flared in my chest, and Ms. Snark escaped from her cage. "Not all that active, if there's no budget to truly investigate."

Will lowered his bowl to the table. "Look, I know you like a good mystery to unravel, but haven't you learned by now that chasing murderers can be dangerous?" There was a hint of snark in his own voice.

The heat rose to flush my cheeks. It was part embarrassment now, because he was right, but I wasn't about to admit that. "The killer's probably long gone by now, like you said, or dead."

"Or alive and well," he shot back, "and living one town over, with friends here who are keeping him informed of our every move."

"Yeah, and how likely is that?" I fired right back.

"Likely enough that I'm tracking down the current whereabouts of the residents back then."

I opened my mouth, but a random thought drove whatever I was about to say right out of my mind. What if Will found Dexter's father? Would that be a good thing or a bad thing?

I brought my mind back to the current conversation, or argument rather. "Why was it okay to talk to Edna and Dexter but not to Sherie?"

Will caught himself mid eye roll. "Because you often go walking in the mornings and run into Edna and chat, so that looked totally natural. And you happened to run into Dexter as well—a bonus. But I'll take it from here."

I stood and grabbed up his bowl, sloshing some of the remaining milk onto the table. "And I also naturally talk to my next-door neighbor. Almost every day, as a matter of fact." I stomped to the sink and dumped the bowl into it.

A sigh from behind me. "How did this end up in an argument?"

My chest hurt as I tried to answer that question for myself. Why was I trying to butt into Will's investigation? Didn't I have enough on my own plate, what with trying to train two dogs at once?

I gave a small shrug without turning around.

"I've got a meeting in Ocala this morning," he said in a carefully neutral voice, "then paperwork to finish up on that other case. I'll probably be back here mid-afternoon, unless something comes up."

I made a show of rinsing the bowl. "Are they going to be able to finish the skating rink?"

Another sigh. "Maybe. A CSI team is coming out today to make sure there are no more bodies out there."

"Okay..." I mentally slapped a hand over my mouth. I'd almost said, *There's my excuse to talk to Sherie.* "Uh, see ya later then."

A hand on my shoulder, tugging. I let him turn me around.

He gave me a gentle smile, then kissed my forehead. "Have a good day."

I returned the smile with a feeble one of my own. "You too."

"Stay out of trouble," he threw over his shoulder as he left the kitchen.

I shook my head. "You just couldn't resist, could you?" I muttered under my breath, once he was out of earshot.

I hoped we didn't end up in the same argument again tonight.

Because I was sure of two things. One, I'd get more out of Sherie than he would. And two, Mayfair was my home now—indeed I felt more at home here than I ever had in Baltimore, where I was born and raised.

If a long-buried secret was going to threaten my new hometown's serenity, then I wanted to be out ahead of it.

CHAPTER FOUR

The morning went by quickly. Working with two dogs who were more or less at the same stage of development was challenging. Normally I had one dog fairly well along when I started the next one. That made the training process more interesting for me, and it also meant I was delivering a trained dog to a client—which is when I get paid—every three months.

But termites had driven me temporarily out of my house toward the end of the summer and interrupted that normal routine. So now I had two dogs at roughly the same stage, although Josie, a fluffy brown mutt with a sweet face, was catching on faster than Rocky.

Josie already knew the pay-attention-you're on-duty signal, a flat palm held out parallel to the ground, signaling she was to touch it with her nose and then keep her mind on the tasks at hand.

I taught it by holding a small treat between the tips of my thumb and index finger while keeping the rest of my hand as flat as possible. The dog would naturally sniff at my hand, trying to find whatever that was that smelled so good.

When their nose would touch the center of my palm, I'd said,

"Good girl," or "Good boy" as the case might be. Then I'd quickly take the treat out from between my fingers with my other hand and give it to the dog.

After doing that a few times, I would hold my hand out flat without the treat. They'd nose it, thinking there must be something good there again. And I'd praise them and give them a treat.

Josie had caught on in one session, but Rocky, a Black Labrador mixed with some breed that was slightly smaller and bulkier, was living down to his name. He was dumb as a rock.

He kept snapping at the treat between my fingers, convinced this was a game. Today I was determined to get through to him.

I took all three dogs out into the backyard at once. I told them to sit, a command they all knew well. Josie and Buddy immediately plopped their butts onto the ground.

Rocky just stood there for a second, wagging his tail.

"Sit, Rocky," I said, in a firm voice, wondering if I'd made a big mistake with my initial assessment of this dog. Black Labs were usually quite bright, even if a little distractible when young. And Rocky had certainly seemed eager to please when I'd first gotten him from the rescue shelter.

"Sit," I said yet again. He finally sat.

"Stay," I said to all of them. Then I held my palm out flat above Buddy's head.

He, of course, touched his nose to my palm. I quickly praised him and reached in my pocket for a treat.

Rocky held his position in line but stood up, his tail wagging tentatively.

"Sit," I barked, then took a deep breath to calm myself.

The dog sat again, but he gave me a confused, almost hurt look.

I brought my hand out without a treat. An idea was forming in my brain.

I held my palm out to Josie and she touched her nose to it.

"Good girl," I said, as I always did to mark the desired behavior, but then I added, with exaggerated enthusiasm, "You are such a good girl."

I held my hand out over Rocky's head. He stood and sniffed my palm.

"Good boy!" He wasn't supposed to stand but I ignored that. We'd deal with that another day.

Instead of producing a food treat, I leaned over and scratched both his ears. "You're such a good boy."

His whole back end wagged and he licked my wrist.

I held my palm out again. He touched it with his nose. Again, I said, "Good boy," to mark the behavior, then enthusiastically petted and praised him.

We repeated this new "game" a dozen times, until he nosed my palm without any hesitation.

Holding onto Rocky's collar, I gestured to Buddy and Josie. "Go lie down." I pointed to the magnolia tree to one side of my yard, about halfway down its length.

Buddy trotted off in that direction. Josie looked at me, then Buddy, and finally followed him.

I worked with Rocky for a few minutes on other simple commands he already knew, then I suddenly stopped moving and held my hand out. He tilted his head to one side for half a second, then touched his nose to my palm.

Eureka, I thought as I praised him. My earlier hunch had been right.

Dogs don't all respond at their best to the same rewards. It depends on what is most important to the dog. Most do well with food treats, but not all are food motivated.

I always use "Good boy" or Good girl" to mark a behavior, *mark* meaning to make it clear that was the behavior I was rewarding. Lots of trainers these days use the clicker system for this purpose, but

Mattie Jones, the woman who'd trained me to be a trainer was old-fashioned.

Rocky usually responded well to the "Good boy" marker, but then didn't seem to truly learn the behavior. My hunch was that the treats actually distracted him and the behavior was forgotten instead of being reinforced. But the marker followed by more elaborate praise was rewarding the behavior for him.

Good to know going forward.

At ten-forty, I stopped for a break, well pleased with the morning's progress.

I gave the dogs fresh water, put several treats in both Josie's and Rocky's bowls and closed their crate doors. Then with Buddy on my heels, I headed out front to knock on Sherie Wells's door.

She wasn't particularly surprised by the news that the lot across from us was still considered a crime scene. Shaking her head, she invited me in and offered iced tea.

I gratefully accepted. She gestured for me to follow her to the kitchen.

"They're going to be looking for more bodies," I said, "for at least today, just in case."

Sherie shuddered and waved her hand toward the kitchen table, an old-fashioned, gray metal one with a red formica top.

I was secretly pleased and honored. This meant I had graduated from a "guest" who sat on the navy velveteen sofa in the living room to a friend.

After she'd populated the table with glasses, sugar bowl, two pitchers, a plate of cookies and one of those long-handled spoons specifically made for iced tea, she placed a dish of water on the floor for Buddy. "I doubt we'll be able to get the ice rink done now anyway," she sat down across from me, "even if they only tie it up for another day or two."

I used the iced-tea spoon to put a little sugar in my glass and then poured tea over it, appreciating that Sherie always remembered my distaste for Southern sweet tea and kept a pitcher of unsweetened on hand especially for me.

I chose my words carefully. "I've been wondering if it was really such a good idea anyway. The costs involved would have offset any increased income from tourists for at least a couple of years." That was being extremely optimistic—more like for a half-dozen years to come. But I was trying not to forfeit my newly achieved kitchen-table status.

Sherie waved a hand in the air, as if flicking away a pesky fly. "That doesn't matter all that much to Edna. She viewed it as long-term investment."

"Edna was bankrolling the whole thing?"

Sherie nodded.

This was news to me, but then I had tuned out for the last part of that meeting.

"She's got a trust fund, set up by her brother."

Also news to me, but it explained a lot. Such as how Edna was able to rebuild her motel much nicer and bigger than the one that had burned down. She'd probably supplemented the insurance settlement from her own funds.

"Dexter's got one too. Edna's the trustee."

"Wow, the alligator farm must have done a booming business in its day."

Sherie shrugged. "It did okay for a few years, but Mr. Mayfair had money even before then. Family money. Still, he had a strong work ethic. Like Edna, he loved being busy with some project, preferably one that made a profit. But if it didn't, that was okay too."

She paused and took a sip of her tea. "And I think Edna feels some responsibility to try to rebuild the town. So she liked your idea of promoting tourism, even if she's not all that into Christmas herself."

"Are you still going to try to do the extravaganza thing?" I winced inside when I heard the *you.* I hoped Sherie hadn't picked up on my attempt to distance myself from the idea. "Without the skating rink, that is?"

"Yes. Edna wants to give it a trial run this year. Advertise the fact that we are a quiet and quaint town, but only a couple of hours from Disney World. Then we'll work on the skating rink for next year."

It actually sounded like a reasonably sane plan. Or had I been hanging out with this crowd for too long?

Not coming up with a better segue, I blurted out, "So what's your theory on the skeleton?"

She shrugged again, a gesture not all that in character for Sherie.

"Thirty years ago," I said, "wasn't that around the time that Dexter's father took off?"

She narrowed her eyes at me for half a second, then quickly smoothed out her expression. "A little before that, if I remember correctly. It was soon after Jason and I moved to Jacksonville and I started teaching."

"Theirs wasn't a very happy marriage, was it? Dexter's parents, I mean."

Sherie dropped her gaze. She didn't answer me, instead busying herself with topping off my iced tea glass, even though she hadn't asked if I wanted more. I suspected this was part of kitchen-table friends.

At the very least it meant she wasn't going to throw me out on my ear for asking nosy questions. So I tried yet again. "And then Dexter's mother got sick right after that. Poor woman. What did she die of?"

Sherie made eye contact, staring at me for a second. Then her expression softened into one of indulgence. But she didn't smile.

I realized she hadn't smiled since greeting me at the front door.

"Susanna was a bit fragile," she said. "Perhaps she was born that way and it was a good thing that her daddy and aunt sheltered her so, or maybe the sheltering was what made her fragile. She and I were friends in elementary school, although not best friends. Or *besties* as my daughter would say." She sighed.

"Then her daddy sent her to private boarding school for high school. Our little high school here wasn't that great."

And now it was closed, as were all the schools. The few kids in town were bussed to Belleview for school, or in some cases, homeschooled.

"She came back three years later," Sherie continued, "married to an 'older' man." She made air quotes. "He was mid-twenties, and her daddy took an instant dislike to him. Mr. Mayfair tried to convince her to divorce the man, or get an annulment, until he found out she was already pregnant."

She poured herself more tea. "He set them up in a small house, gave her housekeeping money, but refused to full-out support them."

Sounded pretty close to full-out support to me. I picked up a cookie and nibbled on it, more to keep my hands and mouth busy so I wouldn't blurt something out and interrupt the flow.

"*That man* drank too much, that was evident from the get-go. But it wasn't until after Dexter was born that it came out he'd been beating Susie."

I noted that Sherie never called Dexter's father by name. He was always "the man" or "*that* man."

"He'd even kicked her in the womb a couple of times," she said. "We think that's why Dexter's a little slow, that he did him some damage before he was born."

I wasn't sure who the *we* stood for, but I kept my mouth shut, chewing on the chocolate chip cookie.

"Then my husband and I moved away. When my babies started coming, my mother would come to help out. She brought me up to date on things back here in Mayfair." She met my gaze, the faraway look in her eyes clearing. Her mouth pinched into a grim line. "It was a dark time for the Mayfairs. Finally that man took off, but Susie didn't deal with it well. Shortly after, she had a nervous breakdown. She went into a mental hospital, and then a private sanitarium."

Sherie's eyes were now shiny with unshed tears. She gave another uncharacteristic shrug.

My throat tightened. "It's gotta be depressing," I said softly, "to have all that stirred up in your memory, because of the skeleton."

She nodded, looked off into space again. "It broke Mr. Mayfair. She was the last of the line. Edna'd never married and his wife had died when Susie was nine. He'd doted on his little girl."

"But wait, she wasn't the last of the line. There was Dexter."

Sherie smiled but her eyes were still clouded with sadness. "It was pretty obvious by the time his mama died that he wasn't completely right in the head. Mr. Mayfair loved him and provided for him, but I don't think he ever thought of him as an heir, even though he arranged with his lawyer to change the boy's name to Mayfair. He didn't want Dexter's last name to be a constant reminder of *that man*. The word got around pretty quick that no one was to ever say his name in Mr. Mayfair's presence ever again."

Sherie gave a slight shake of her head. "Mr. Mayfair died shortly after Dexter turned eight, just a year and a half after Susanna's death. Doctor said he had a massive heart attack, but my mama said it was really a broken heart that killed him."

We sat quietly for a couple of beats while I processed all that. "If Susanna had a mental illness," I asked, "what did she die from?"

Sherie's eyes widened some. She shook her head slightly again and a tear broke loose.

I thought she wasn't going to answer me. But then she did.

"Susie committed suicide."

CHAPTER FIVE

I knew I was treading on dangerous ground by telling Will about my conversation with Sherie. But I couldn't *not* tell him. The info might be relevant to his investigation.

He hadn't made it home until dinnertime, and he'd brought Chinese as a peace offering.

I took a deep breath and plunged in. "I saw Sherie today."

He paused, a chunk of General Tso's chicken snagged between chopsticks and halfway to his mouth.

I never could master those dang things. I twisted some lo mein noodles onto my fork. "What?" I said in response to his raised eyebrows. "She invited me in for tea."

Liar, liar, pants on fire, Ms. Snark quipped inside my head.

It's a half truth, not a lie, I answered silently.

And besides Will was buying it. His rugged, tanned face had relaxed and his baby blues were no longer drilling holes in my face. "What'd she have to say?" He popped the chicken into his mouth and chewed.

I told him the long, sad story while we ate.

When I got to the final tidbit—Dexter's mother's suicide—Will looked a little startled.

But not as much so as I had been that morning. Now I wondered why I hadn't seen it coming. After all, Sherie had begun the whole story with "Susanna was fragile."

"Do you think any of this has anything to do with your skeleton?" I asked.

He shrugged. "Hard to say, but I should probably try to find out more. I wonder which mental hospital she was in."

"If Dexter's theory has merit," I said as I cracked open a fortune cookie, "that his father killed somebody and that's why he took off, Susanna might have known something about it. Maybe there's something in her counseling records about what happened back then."

I read the fortune and grimaced.

"Maybe," Will said. "I'll ask Edna for the name of the hospital. I wanted to talk to her again anyway. I think she knows more about all this than she's telling."

He reached for a fortune cookie. "What's your fortune say?"

I waved a hand in the air. "You know they're not really fortunes anymore, just generic pronouncements. The Chinese don't even have fortune cookies. They're an American invention."

Will grinned at me. "You always say that when you don't like your fortune. Come on, what is it?"

I shook my head and reached for the slip of paper I'd dropped on the table.

But Will's hand snaked out and snatched it up. He smoothed it out and read it aloud. "Your curiosity is both your greatest asset and your worst liability."

He threw back his head and laughed out loud.

❄

It was destined to be a week of surprises. Old skeletons surfacing, then Sherie's news about Susanna Mayfair's suicide, and now Will had agreed to let me tag along when he went to visit the sanitarium where she had resided, some thirty plus years ago.

He'd gone to talk to Edna first thing this morning and had come home in a grim mood.

"What'd she say?" I asked.

"She acknowledged the suicide. Her exact words were 'I figgered Marcia'd ferret out that bit of gossip.'" He did a credible job of imitating Edna's creaky, irritated voice. "And I eventually got the name of the place her niece was sent to. It's a private 'hospital.'" He made air quotes. "But she wouldn't say anything else. Insisted it was in the past and should stay there."

As to the issue of me going along when he investigated this private hospital, Will wasn't even that hard a sell. I'd made the points that it would hardly be dangerous and that I might be able to get more out of the nurses than he could, but I really think his caving was more about how little time we'd had together recently, because of his big drug case that was no longer his.

I'd had a quick but successful training session with Rocky while Will had been talking to Edna, so I only felt a little guilty about taking off for part of the day. I left my trainees in their crates with fresh water and chew toys. Buddy had the run of the house though.

Once we were settled in his car, I said, "I'm kind of surprised that Edna wouldn't tell you more. She's usually pretty respectful of authority."

Will grimaced, as he turned the steering wheel to negotiate the curve in front of the motel. "Downside of being the resident cop. People aren't as afraid of you. They assume you'll give them a pass because you know them."

I hid a smile. "Well, didn't you give her a pass?"

He grimaced again. "What was I supposed to do? Haul her into

Ocala to the sheriff's department and grill her in an interview room?"

I chuckled. "That would have pissed her off royally, that you'd interrupted her work. You would've gotten squat then."

"That's what I figured." He turned north on US 301.

"Speaking of Ocala, is that where we're headed?"

He nodded but then said, "Belleview."

I grinned. Belleview was one of my favorite towns in Marion County. A small community adjoining the southern side of Ocala, most folks didn't even know it was a separate entity from the bigger city.

For the most part, it felt like a suburb of Ocala, but there were still remnants of its old, small-town charm, if you knew where to look.

One such remnant was the street we ended up on. The only thing that differentiated our destination from the other rambling old houses on the shady block was a discreet wooden sign. It read, *Sunny Palms Retirement Center*. Will pulled to the curb in front of it.

I hopped out and stood on the sidewalk looking around, while Will circled the parked car and joined me. There was very little sunshine peeking through the dense canopy of ancient live oaks, and not a palm tree in sight.

"Sunny Palms?" I said in a low voice as we walked to the front porch.

Will snorted.

"Did you call ahead?" I asked.

"Nope. Sometimes the element of surprise is useful." The front door opened as we stepped up onto a large wooden porch. An elderly gentleman, in a threadbare flannel shirt and corduroys that bagged on him, stood in the doorway. He didn't speak, just smiled and stepped back, holding the door open for us to enter.

I assumed he was a resident, and Will must have made the same assumption. He thanked the man and walked past him. I followed, exchanging a pleasant nod with the old fellow.

We were in a large entrance hall, made dark with hardwood floors and mahogany paneling. It had a rich feel to it until one noticed the peeling paint on the ceiling and the scars on both the floor and walls.

In the center of the hall, a small sign in a metal stand told us that visitors must check in at the reception desk.

We parted to walk around either side of the sign, and I spotted the desk farther down the hallway. It too was scarred mahogany and massive, covered with piles of papers.

A middle-aged woman—on the plump side, well-dressed, with a cap of short gray curls surrounding a pasty face—sat behind it. She looked up as we approached and gave us a big welcoming smile. "Can I help you?" Her teeth were too even. Dentures perhaps.

Will flashed his badge. "Detective Haines, ma'am. Marion County Sheriff's Department." He didn't introduce me.

The smile only faltered a little and something flickered in her eyes, too quick for me to name it. "How can I help you, Detectives?"

Will let the plural slide. "How long have you worked here, Miss…?"

"Mrs. Beckett," she said, still with a smile, although not quite as wide. "I'm the owner. I worked for the woman who opened this place, then bought it from her when she wanted to retire."

Her words sounded helpful but she really hadn't answered Will's question. Giving him a wide-eyed innocent stare, she looked like somebody's grandmother.

She probably is *somebody's grandmother, but that doesn't mean she isn't up to something*, suspicious Ms. Snark observed.

Will gave Mrs. Beckett a charming smile. "And when did you start working for the previous owner?"

"In 1980. I was fresh out of secretarial school. Ellen Brooks took me under her wing and taught me all about hospital administration."

"Good," Will said. "Then perhaps you remember someone who

was here in the early to mid eighties, Susanna Hill? Or she might have been admitted under the name of Mayfair."

Another flicker. Anxiety?

"Um, Sunny Palms was a private hospital then, so admissions would be confidential."

"But you do remember Susanna?" Will's tone was a bit sterner than it had been.

She straightened her back. "I'm afraid I can't comment on a patient from that era."

Will let out an exaggerated sigh. "Please don't make me get a subpoena. She's long dead, after all."

Mrs. Beckett's expression was not hard to read this time. Total surprise. But she quickly wiped her face clean and gave Will a blank stare. Her brown eyes were hard as marbles. "Confidentiality does not die with the patient."

"So she did die," Will said, "while she was a patient here?"

Now something clouded the woman's face. Confusion? Indecision?

"If she didn't die here," Will's voice was clipped with irritation, "then where did she die?"

Mrs. Beckett's gaze flicked down the hall and then quickly back to us.

There's something down there she doesn't want us to see. I opened my mouth to say something, but Will had caught the furtive glance.

He placed his knuckles on the edge of the desk and leaned forward, crowding Mrs. Beckett's space. "What are you hiding?" he said in a low, even tone.

Dang, he was good. I'd be confessing to every crime ever committed if he got in my face that way.

Then a crazy thought hit me so hard it literally had me reeling backward a step. I grabbed Will's sleeve to steady myself, but my eyes were on Mrs. Beckett. "She isn't dead, is she?"

CHAPTER SIX

Will turned to me, his eyebrows halfway to his hairline, his mouth slightly open. Then he pivoted toward the hallway and started down it at a brisk pace.

Mrs. Beckett jumped up and rounded her desk. "Hey, you can't go down there. Those are residents' private rooms."

Will ignored her and kept walking.

Mrs. Beckett ran to get in front of him. Her face even paler than it had been, she held up a hand. "Don't! You'll scare her."

Will stopped.

She took a deep breath and let it out slowly, her shoulders slumping. "I'll get her. Wait in the conference room." She pointed to a nearby door.

The strands of gray were barely noticeable in the long strawberry-blonde hair of the woman sitting across from us at the conference table. Her face was remarkably smooth. Only the distended veins on the hands folded demurely in front of her matched her sixty-something age.

Meanwhile, Mrs. Beckett was wringing *her* hands, while standing in the small conference room's doorway.

"Thank you, Mrs. Beckett," Will said, his voice dismissive. "We'll let you know if we have more questions for you." Apparently he'd decided to go with her assumption that I was also a cop, his partner.

Mrs. Beckett continued to hover. Will shot her a look and she finally left.

He nodded to me. "Get the door."

I got up from the table—more scarred mahogany—and closed the door. It was also wooden but newer and pine-colored, with a small window in it. I wondered if Mrs. Beckett would try to spy on us. I resumed my seat next to Will.

"Mrs. Hill," he said to the woman across from us.

She didn't respond.

"Ms. Mayfair?"

Still no response.

On a hunch, I said, "Susie?"

She turned her head toward me. "Yes?" Her voice was so low, I wondered if I'd just imagined that she'd spoken.

She wore a dark blue dress with a pattern of tiny pink flowers. It hung on her and was years out of date, but seemed to be of good quality. Plucking at the fabric of the cuff around her wrist, she said, "Who are you?" Her tone was mildly curious.

I forced a relaxed smile, even though my chest was so tight it was hard to breathe. "A friend of your Aunt Edna's."

Her face brightened. "Aunt Edna? Is she here?"

"No." I kept my voice gentle. "I'll bring her to see you soon, okay?"

"Yes, please. That would be great."

"Susie," Will said, "how long have you been here?"

Her sky-blue eyes widened slightly. "In this room?" She sounded like maybe she thought it was a trick question.

"Here at Sunny Palms," Will said.

She tilted her head to one side. "I'm not sure. A long time. It's where I live now."

The last sentence had a practiced feel to it. I wondered if it had been repeated to her over and over until she no longer questioned its veracity.

My throat tightened and my eyes stung. I glanced at Will.

His face was devoid of emotion, only the deepening of the furrow between his brows giving away the effort involved in keeping it that way.

I'd make a lousy cop. I swallowed hard.

Will had gotten her talking about her days here.

"It's an okay place to live," she said in response to one of his questions. "I don't have anywhere else to go."

I opened my mouth. Will shot me a look and I slammed it shut again.

"Who brought you here?" Will asked.

"My father, although I don't remember it very well. I was really sick then and he said I needed to be in the hospital for a while." She paused, glanced down, plucked again at her sleeve. "He's dead now. Died three years ago, or was it four?"

I swallowed hard again. Mr. Mayfair had been dead for over two decades.

She brightened again. "Tuesday and Thursday afternoons are the best. The OT comes then. He teaches us how to make stuff for poor kids."

"What kind of stuff?" Will asked.

"Oh, little sweaters and caps for orphaned babies. And some people are allowed to whittle the toy trucks and trains for the older boys." She ducked her head. "I'm not allowed to have the whittlin' knife though, 'cause I used to cut on myself, back when I was depressed."

Thus the long sleeves. They probably hid scars.

"When were you depressed?" Will asked.

"Oh, years ago." She threw a hand in the air as if flicking off the pesky memory. "But I'm okay now, as long as I take my pills." Pluck, pluck at her sleeve. "Nurse Karen didn't come yet today. I hope she isn't sick. I hate it when they send another nurse."

Will softly cleared his throat, the only indicator that this interview was getting to him. "Why is that?" he asked in a gentle voice.

"The other nurses don't want to sit and talk first. They just stand over me and watch me take the pills."

"But Karen talks first?"

"Yeah, it's the best part of the day. I get to talk to someone, as if I were normal again."

Tears stung and threatened to erupt. I grasped the sides of my chair's seat and dug my fingernails into the wood underneath. I knew if I got up and fled the room, as I wanted to do, it would break the precious rhythm of the interview.

"But on Tuesdays and Thursdays," Will said, "the OT comes. Is that an occupational therapist?"

She stared at him for a beat. "I guess. I never really thought about it. Everybody calls him the OT, or Jim. That's his name. I'm usually okay enough by the afternoons to participate." She looked around a bit nervously. "I hope Nurse Karen gets here soon. Otherwise I'll be too out of it when Jim comes."

She turned back to Will. "It is Thursday, isn't it?"

The door swung open. "Sorry to interrupt," Mrs. Beckett said, not sounding the least bit sorry. "But the nurse is here to give Ms. Mayfair her meds. They're already overdue."

Will reached across the table and patted Susie's hand. She

flinched a little but didn't pull away. "Thanks for talking to me, Susie. I'll come visit again, if that's okay with you?"

"Oh, yes. I'd like that." Susanna Mayfair gave Will a bright smile.

She turned to me. "Nice meeting you, uh…"

"Marcia," I said.

"Mar-see-a." She said each syllable distinctly, a slight note of glee in her voice. "What a lovely name."

My heart burst inside my chest. I bit down on my lower lip to keep the tears at bay. "Thanks. Nice meeting you too. I'll bring Aunt Edna to see you soon."

She clapped her hands, smiling again, then let Mrs. Beckett lead her from the room.

Will exited right behind and followed the two women down the hall. I trailed along, hanging back, still fighting tears.

Another woman, blonde and fortyish, in blue scrubs, stood by an open doorway. She wore too much makeup and her face was pinched. She looked like she'd been sucking on a lemon, maybe a rotten one.

I'd hoped Will was planning on hauling Susanna Mayfair out of there, but he reached for Mrs. Beckett's elbow instead and deftly inserted himself between her and her charge. He let the nurse lead Susanna into her room.

"I have some more questions for you, ma'am." His words were polite but his tone was hard. "Marcia, wait here for the nurse. Tell her we need to talk to her before she leaves."

He led a spluttering Mrs. Beckett back toward the small conference room.

Thirty minutes later, two uniformed deputies had arrived and were now standing at parade rest next to the reception desk. Mrs. Beckett was back in her chair behind it. Will had given the uniforms lengthy, hushed instructions. From the few words I'd caught, they were to make sure Mrs. Beckett stayed put and didn't mess with any of the records.

Then Will made a show of walking around the desk—Mrs. Beckett cringed away from him in her chair—and pulling the plug of the small shredder behind it from the wall socket.

He beckoned to me and the nurse to follow and headed for the conference room. Once we were settled around the table, he pulled out a small pad and poised his pen over it. "Name?" he barked.

"Bella Stevens." Her face was blank. Too blank. But there was definitely a hint of anxiety in her eyes as they flicked about the room.

"And you work for?"

"Belleview Nightingales. It's a nursing and caretaker service."

Will nodded, one sharp movement of his head down and up. "What meds is Ms. Mayfair receiving?"

"Can't tell you that," Nurse Bella said. "Patient confidentiality."

"Harumph." Will stared at her. "Name of the doctor who ordered the meds?"

Aha, that would not be confidential.

She froze for a second, then said, "Dr. Nelson."

Will wrote the name down. "And he is what, a psychiatrist?"

She glanced at me, swallowed hard. "No, I believe he's a general practitioner."

"And when was the last time the order was renewed?"

"Um, I don't know. I'd have to check the patient's chart."

"Which is kept where?"

"In Mrs. Beckett's file cabinet."

Will looked at me and gave a small nod. I took that to mean I was to go fetch the chart.

Once outside the conference room door, I took a deep breath and squared my shoulders. Acting had never been my greatest talent, but I was about to pretend I had the authority to do what I was about to do.

I marched to Mrs. Beckett's desk, then veered off to the filing cabinet to its left. The only labels on the drawers were alphabetical designations—A-L, etc.—except for the bottom drawer. I opened the M-Q drawer.

"Hey, you can't go in there," Mrs. Beckett called out.

I turned slightly and gave her what I hoped was a quelling look.

"Don't you need a search warrant?" she said more tentatively.

I hid a grin. Guess my look had been quelling enough.

"The nurse needs Ms. Mayfair's chart," I said in a curt voice. I'd located the M's and quickly rifled through them. There it was: *Mayfair, Susanna*. I pulled out the chart and turned.

"You can't look at that without a court order," Mrs. Beckett said more emphatically.

"I have no intention of looking at it." Actually, I had planned to sneak a peek. "The nurse needs it to check something."

"What?"

I resisted the temptation to say, *None of your business.*

Instead, I gestured for her to follow me. "You can tag along to make sure I don't open it." I turned and walked away, Mrs. Beckett spluttering behind me.

I was relieved to see out of the corner of my eye that a uniform was also tagging along. He would keep tabs on Mrs. Beckett, make sure she returned to her desk.

When I stepped back into the conference room, Will's hands were in the air in a gesture of frustration. "Look, I know–" He broke off when he saw Mrs. Beckett.

I made a show of handing the file to the nurse, then made shooing motions at Mrs. Beckett. She reluctantly stepped back and I closed the door in her face.

When I turned back, Will's face was neutral but there was a twinkle in his eye as he met mine. "I know you can't tell me what the meds are," he said to the nurse, "but I need to determine if Ms.

Mayfair needs some kind of counter-dose to whatever you just gave her."

Nurse Bella pulled back, her shoulders stiffening. "Of course not. They're properly prescribed psychotropic drugs in appropriate doses."

"For what?" I blurted out. "To keep a woman so doped up she doesn't even realize she's being held captive?"

Will shot me a look, but it wasn't as censoring as it could have been. He pointed to the chart. "The doctor's order?"

Nurse Bella rifled through the pages. She looked up, her face now slightly flushed. "Um, it is a bit out of date, but it's not my job to get it renewed."

"How out of date?" Will's voice was sharp.

"Two months. I told Mrs. Beckett last time I was here that it was about to expire."

He leaned a little bit forward. "It *is* your job to check the order, is it not, *before* you administer the meds?"

Suddenly Nurse Bella's face crumpled. "Please, I'll lose my license. I always hate it when they send me here."

"Why's that?" His tone was now almost conversational.

She shook her head slightly. "I've suspected something fishy for a while."

"Fishy how?"

"If I tell you, can we keep it between us?" She glanced desperately from Will to me and back again. "I'm a single mom, with teenagers. I need this job."

"I can't make any guarantees but I'll report that you were very cooperative."

She sat back and sighed. Tears were making ugly tracks in her makeup, streaking her mascara. "I've told my supervisor twice that I don't think some of the patients here need the meds they're on. She says the agency checked into it and the doctor's orders are valid. And that's all we can do, according to her. It's not our place to question the doctor's decisions regarding their patients."

"How many patients, and they have different doctors?"

"Five, and no, they're all patients of Dr. Lucas Nelson."

"Okay, Ms. Stevens," Will said. "I'm going to overlook the fact that you gave the patient her meds before checking the doctor's order to see if it had been renewed. I'll have more questions for you though, so I need your home address and phone number."

With a look of relief on her face, the woman rattled off that information. Will wrote it down.

"Please don't tell anyone about our conversation." His tone conveyed that it was an order, not a request.

"Not even my supervisor?"

"*Especially* not your supervisor. And Ms. Stevens," he leaned forward in a confiding manner, "you might want to start looking for another job. Your agency may very well not exist when all this is over."

She blanched, then nodded. "May I go?"

He gestured toward the door, where I was still standing. I stepped aside and she fled.

"What happens now?" I asked.

Will gave a slight shake of his head. "Don't know for sure. I have to call the health department. They're the ones who oversee licensure of places like this. And I need to contact the next of kin of those who seem to be overmedicated. If they have power of attorney, they can give permission to see the patients' records."

He heaved a sigh and slumped down in his chair. "What a mess. You should probably take my car and go home. I may be here all day. But don't tell anyone about this yet."

I stepped over to him and laid a hand on his shoulder, gave it a squeeze. In truth, the contact was as much for my own comfort as his. "Not even Edna?" I said quietly.

"Definitely not Edna. I want to see her face when she hears the news that her niece is still alive."

"I'm glad you took it easy on the nurse."

Will patted my hand and turned his head to give me a small smile. "Not checking the doctor's order first was really her only breach. She's right about the rest. Nurses aren't supposed to question a doctor's order. It's the doctor and the nursing agency that I want."

His face hardened, a sharp gleam in his eye that I'd never seen before. "And Mrs. Beckett."

CHAPTER SEVEN

Edna's eyes and mouth made three big O's on her face, reminding me of the Wow emoji on Facebook.

And I was very glad that I had abided by Will's instructions. Witnessing her expression had to prove to him that she knew nothing about the arrangements regarding her niece.

Mind you, it had been difficult to keep myself from racing to the motel and blurting it out. I'd hid in the backyard with the dogs, but I'd not been all that attentive to their training. I'd reinforced what they already knew, without attempting to introduce anything new.

"You had no idea she was still alive?" Will said.

Edna shook her head and the tears pooling in her eyes broke loose. "I knew John had set up a trust fund," she snuffled into a tissue she pulled from a pocket in her old brown sweater.

With a pang, I remembered that the sweater had belonged to her brother.

"To pay her medical expenses," she continued. "He did the ones for me and Dexter at the same time. But I assumed he'd dismantled that one when she died." She sniffed and her lip trembled.

I reached out and took her hand. She and I were sitting on the sofa in the motel's sitting room, Buddy at my feet. Will sat across from us in an antique wingback armchair.

He leaned forward, elbows on his knees. "Why do you think your brother told you she was dead?"

Her lips pinched together. "Dang good question."

The anger in her voice set off a wave of relief inside of me. Edna might be shocked but she hadn't lost her feisty.

"Maybe the doctors back then told him she was incurable…" Will shot me a quelling look, which I ignored. "And he figured thinking she was dead would make it easier for everyone to grieve and then move on."

It was the only logical explanation, and John Mayfair hadn't expected to drop dead himself so soon after that.

"Where is my niece?" Edna demanded. "I want to see her."

"Tonight?" I asked. It was after six.

"Yes." Her tone was emphatic. "It's a visit already thirty years overdue."

"She's at Ocala General." Will stood up. "I'll take you."

"Shouldn't we tell Dexter first?" I asked.

"No," Edna said, her voice firm. "I need to see what kinda shape Susanna's in before we involve the boy."

I was tempted to point out that "the boy" was pushing forty but I restrained myself. Instead I said, "He has a right to know."

Will pursed his lips. "I think Edna's right. And I'm not sure that Susanna's up for too much reality all at once."

Suddenly Edna burst into tears and buried her face in her hands.

I wrapped an arm around her shoulders. "I'm going with," I mouthed to Will.

He nodded, his face grim.

❄

The visit actually ended up being a bit anticlimactic, for me at least.

A nurse led us to Susanna's room. She had been given a mild sedative to help her sleep in a strange, and for her, probably scary environment. She was groggy when we got there.

But she recognized Edna and gave her a beatific if sleepy smile.

Edna stroked the gray-blonde hair back from her niece's forehead. "You rest, sweetie. I'll come back tomorrow."

The nurse gestured for us to follow her to a small lounge area. She carried a clipboard under her arm.

"Are you Ms. Mayfair's closest kin?" she asked Edna, once we were all settled on the stiff vinyl-covered chairs.

Edna hesitated only a fraction of a second. I'm not sure anyone but me even caught it. Technically Dexter was next of kin, but Edna nodded.

"The health department has authorized emergency care for her," the nurse handed over the clipboard and a pen, "but we need authorization to continue her treatment as needed."

Edna's gaze scanned the page on top, her lips moving slightly. Finally she said, "What's this mean, 'reduce medications and treat withdrawal symptoms?'"

"We need to take her off of everything they have her on, so we can assess what is really going on. But some of the meds need to be eased off slowly so she doesn't have a negative reaction."

"Who's her doctor?" Edna demanded.

The nurse smiled. "Dr. Butler. He's very competent. I can set up a time for you to talk to him tomorrow."

"Do that," Edna said as she signed at the bottom of the page.

"Um," the nurse said, "I hate to bring this up but the business office will need to know about payment."

"She has a trust fund, although I have no idea who the trustee is. We thought…" Edna stopped, took a deep breath. "We thought she was dead."

"We can find out the trustee's name," Will spoke up for the first time, "from the records at the… that place."

I wasn't surprised he didn't know what to call it. He'd told us on the way to Ocala that the place wasn't licensed as anything now. It had been once upon a time, as a private hospital, but when the regulations for such establishments were tightened up, they'd changed the facility's status to a boarding house and the nursing agency had taken over any actual medical care authorized by the residents' doctors.

"Why didn't they just become a nursing home?" I'd asked.

"Probably didn't want that much oversight," Will said grimly. "Didn't want anyone to discover they were keeping people drugged up at the behest of their rich families."

Then he'd realized what he'd said and tried to backpedal.

Edna had interrupted him. "No need to pussyfoot around what John did, Will."

Now the nurse looked a little shocked. "You thought she was dead?"

"We were told she'd committed suicide," Edna said, bitterness in her voice.

The nurse nodded. "There were two suicide attempts, according to the medical records, in the first two years she was there. Then they increased her meds to the point where it was lucky she remembered her own name." There was a touch of bitterness in her voice as well.

She had a bit more paperwork to be filled out. "I'll be back tomorrow," Edna said when she'd signed the last sheet.

As we headed for the elevators, she asked, "Can we stop at the gift shop. I'd like to order some flowers so when she wakes up in the mornin', she knows we're thinkin' of her. I don't want her to feel all alone never again." Her voice choked up some on the last few words.

Will agreed while I tried to swallow the huge lump that had suddenly grown in my throat.

Edna, no doubt, had felt pretty alone herself, all those years she was raising her great nephew on her own and dealing with the special challenges he faced.

But the gift shop was closed. We were about to turn away when I spotted something in the plate-glass window.

"Will," I said softly and pointed it out.

A pink knit sweater and cap for a newborn, with the words *Sunny Palms Gifts* in gold on the cellophane bag covering it. Nearby were a wooden train engine and a dump truck, brightly painted, both with *Sunny Palms Gifts* stamped on their cab roofs.

Will swore under his breath, then took my elbow to catch up with Edna, who was already at the hospital's sliding glass entrance doors.

Will called me the next day mid-morning. I'd just taken a break between training sessions and was back out in the yard, about to start working with Rocky. But I answered the call anyway, anxious for any news of Susanna.

I gave the dog the hand signal to lie down, my hand stretched out flat and then lowered toward the ground. Amazingly, Rocky sank down on his belly immediately. I was feeling much better about this guy. He was going to work out after all.

Will was talking in my ear. "Mrs. Beckett finally admitted that they were selling the residents' handicrafts but she claims they got a portion of the proceeds, put in their incidentals funds."

"That's not what Susanna told us. She seemed to think she was making things for poor orphans."

"She may have gotten confused, or Beckett's lying through her teeth."

"I'll take bets on the latter," I said.

Will made a sound, half snort, half laugh. "We've got a forensic accountant going over the books. I suspect we're going to have lots to charge Beckett with when he's done."

"How's Susanna doing?"

"I'm about to go over to the hospital now and check on her. If her head's cleared some, I may be able to ask her some questions."

"Any news on the skeleton?"

A pause.

"Come on, Will. I won't tell anybody."

A soft sigh. "Ollie Tolliver says it's been in the ground thirty to thirty-five years."

I winced at the abuse of the poor man's name.

"Can't get any closer than that without more sophisticated, and expensive, testing," Will was saying. "Definitely male and Caucasian. The mark on the skull he says was made by an axe blade or machete, maybe a shovel. Too thick and deep to be a knife edge. And it's rounded, deeper in the middle than on the ends."

"Was there anything he could get DNA from?"

"I doubt it. The bones were pretty clean. Not sure it would help us much anyway. DNA testing wasn't even in use until the mid 80s."

A sudden thought blurted out of my mouth before I could stop it. "You could compare it to Dexter's."

Another brief pause. "I'd already thought of that possibility, that the skeleton might be his father. I've been trying to track down the man's dental records, but who knows if, when or where he went to the dentist."

"Edna might know." I wasn't sure if I should hope that the skeleton was or wasn't Dexter's father. He seemed to crave an explanation for his father's desertion, especially since that event had triggered his mother's mental illness. But would he feel better if it turned out his father had been murdered?

Then another thought made my stomach roil. What if Susanna killed her husband, and that's what had sent her over the edge?

"I asked Edna," Will was saying in my ear. "She claims she doesn't know if he ever went to the dentist while living in Mayfair, but I'm not sure I trust anything she says anymore. And get this, the skeleton had rather extensive work done at some point, on his lower jaw. He had a partial plate with two implants on either end. And Doc Tolliver says they are a type of implant that was still experimental in the late 1960s to early 1970s."

"Sounds like all that would have been expensive." Something was niggling at the back of my brain.

"Yeah, the doc's checking it out for me, to see who in Florida might have been doing some of those experiments back then."

The thought I was trying to capture skittered away again... *Crapola!*

Something Dexter had said about his father.

"Marcia, you there?"

"Yeah, I was thinking about..." The thought pranced by. I lassoed it and dragged it into the open. "His dad's knuckles. Dexter said his dad had black marks on his knuckles. I assumed at the time that it was ingrained dirt, from whatever kind of work he did. But I got the impression from Sherie that he didn't work for a living once he was married to Dexter's mom. He let Mr. Mayfair support them."

"Could've been tattoos," Will said.

"Could be. That would help explain Edna's and her brother's instant dislike of him. Tattoos weren't nearly as accepted then as they are now."

"That gives me an idea."

"What?"

"Never mind," Will said. "I'll let you know if it pans out."

He signed off abruptly and I stood glaring at my phone.

It buzzed in my hand. Becky calling.

I let it go to voicemail, then texted her, *Training, call you later.*

I could have talked to her for a few minutes. Rocky had fallen asleep, his chin on his paws.

But I knew if I did that I'd probably break my promise to Will. It was really hard for me to keep anything from Becky.

After forty-five minutes, I cut my training session with Rocky short. I was having trouble concentrating, unable to get the image of Susanna in that sterile hospital room out of my head.

Sitting at my kitchen table, I called Will. The call went straight to voicemail. I tried the motel's phone. On the fourth ring, a click, then Edna's voice, sounding pleasant and folksy, "Thank ya for callin' the Mayfair Motel. We've stepped away from the desk right now but we do want to talk to y'all. Please leave a message and we'll call back as soon as we can."

Edna not being there didn't surprise me, but I wondered where Dexter was. Had she told him about his mother and they'd gone together to the hospital?

That was likely. I should probably wait awhile until they came home.

Ha! Patience has never been one of my virtues.

I looked at Buddy, who was watching me from the middle of the room, his head cocked.

"I think I'm going to take myself out to lunch, in Ocala."

Buddy just tilted his head the other way.

As I swung my car past the motel on the way out of town, the place was deserted. No cars in the parking lot, no sign of life around the building or grounds.

A little over an hour later—I'd made a quick stop at a fast food place—I was walking down the hallway to Susanna's room in Ocala General.

The same nurse from last night was coming from the other direction. "Are you here to see Ms. Mayfair?" she said, stopping in front of me.

Her tone was pleasant enough but I had a bad feeling. "Yes, I wanted to make sure she was doing okay."

The nurse's expression could best be described as odd. "She's doing as well as we'd expected."

"Can I see her?"

"Her aunt was here earlier, and that detective too. She's pretty tired."

"I won't stay long."

I tried to move past her but she stepped into my path. "It would be better if you came back later."

Short of forcing my way past her, I had little choice. "Okay."

But it really wasn't okay. I'd come all this way. And the nurse's odd reactions had my stomach queasy with worry.

I went back the way I'd come, walking slowly and glancing over my shoulder every few steps.

The nurse turned down an intersecting hallway. I backtracked and peeked around the corner. She was at a nurses' station, on the phone, her back to me.

I scooted across to the other corridor and power-walked to Susanna's door. I opened it partway and stuck my head in.

She lay under a white blanket, her face turned away from the door. There were no wires or tubes hooked up to her. A good sign, I assumed. She seemed to be sleeping.

I was about to withdraw my head, when she moaned. Then a muffled noise that sounded like, "No, no."

I slipped into the room and tiptoed to the bed.

Her eyes were closed but her arms, lying on top of the blanket, were twitching. Her lips moved slightly and she moaned again.

Should I wake her? She seemed to be having a bad dream.

Her eyes suddenly opened and her head jerked in my direction.

I jumped, one hand flying to my chest.

She grabbed my other hand with both of hers. “Aunt Edna, I’m so sorry.”

Heart still pounding, I patted her hand. “It’s okay, Susie. You were dream–”

“It was awful,” she choked out, tears welling in her blue eyes. Then she abruptly closed them and let go of my hand.

“So awful.” She started swinging her fists back and forth, as if she were pummeling someone. “Hit him, get him, hit him,” she chanted.

I stood frozen beside the bed.

She lifted both hands together, high in the air. At first, I thought she was praying or something, but she brought the hands down in a karate-type chop against her own legs under the blanket. “Stop him!” she yelled.

Her eyes flew open again and she stared at me. Then she screamed at the top of her lungs.

CHAPTER EIGHT

I've had a lot of things happen to me through the years, including being kidnapped, shot at, and fighting off an alligator, but getting thrown out of a hospital was a new, and not very pleasant, experience.

I slunk away with my tail between my legs, figuratively speaking.

Halfway home, my phone rang. I held my breath until the name came up on the Bluetooth screen on my dash, afraid the hospital had called Edna and she was about to give me an earful.

I blew out air when *Will* flashed up on the screen, and I answered the call.

"Hey Marcia," he sounded excited. "We've got an ID. Your tattoo lead paid off."

Normally I would be ecstatic to have him acknowledge I'd contributed to an investigation, but all I felt was dread lying in my stomach like a brick.

"You there?" Will said.

"Yeah, so who does our skeleton belong to?"

"You'd guessed it. He is, or rather was, Dexter's father. Doc Tolliver got the old dental records from the state prison in Starke. In the mid 70s, the university's dental school had the students practicing the new implant techniques on the prisoners. Bartholomew Hill, aka Bart Howard, aka Howard Bartholomew spent three years there, from 1974 to 1977, for insurance fraud and passing bogus checks."

"In other words," I said, "he was a con man."

"Yup, a con man who got into a prison yard brawl and had most of his bottom teeth knocked out. Then he got a free partial plate in exchange for being the dental school's guinea pig. He got out on parole three months before he married Susanna Mayfair. The tattoos on his knuckles are fairly common prison tats, the letters L-O-V-E on one hand and H-A-T-E on the other."

"Sheez, no wonder Edna and her brother were freaked when Susanna brought him home."

"Yeah. He no doubt married her for her money." Will's voice, coming from the speaker, now sounded tight, angry. "Probably thought he would be set for life."

"Instead, he's stuck in a tiny town in the middle of nowhere with just enough money for groceries."

"So he took his frustration out on his poor, young wife," Will said.

The brick in my stomach flipped over. For a few seconds, I thought I would have to pull to the side of the road and throw up.

"Uh, did you talk to Edna today?" It was a feeble attempt to get his mind off of Susanna, which didn't work.

"No, I haven't seen her, but I did check on Susanna. She's not making much sense yet. Her doc doesn't know if the drug cocktail they had her on is still confusing her thinking, or if she really is crazy and perhaps needs some of those drugs."

I found myself praying for the latter. She probably wouldn't be prosecuted for murder if the mental illness diagnosis was confirmed.

"Don't wait dinner on me tonight," Will was saying. "I'll probably be pretty late getting back. We're still trying to sort out the mess at that place. Most of the residents seem to be legitimate elderly boarders, but there are a half dozen of them who were brought there by their parents years ago because they had some kind of mental problem. Beckett and that doctor she's in cahoots with convinced their families to set up trust funds to cover their care. No doubt the parents thought they were seeing that their adult children, who couldn't care for themselves, were going to be okay in the future. And in some cases, it probably was a good set-up. One man there was a menopause baby, born when his mother was fifty. He has Down Syndrome and his parents have been dead now for ten years. But a few of them, like Susanna, maybe could've been helped by more recent developments in treatments."

Pressure had been building in my chest while Will talked. "But the parents had died," I spit out, "and Beckett kept those poor people drugged up so they didn't know what was going on."

In my anger, I'd unintentionally pressed down on the accelerator. I went into a curve and had to slam on the brakes. My tires squealed.

"What was that?"

"Nothing. I hit a curve a little too fast."

A beat of silence. "I'll tell you the rest when I get home."

I took a deep breath. "No, I'm okay. What else?"

"Beckett's claiming she was just trying to help the families deal with hopeless situations, but she was raking in several thousand a month from those trust funds. We found an offshore account with two million dollars stashed in it."

"Not a fortune by today's standards, but a nice retirement nest egg."

"Yeah, well the State of Florida will be financing her retirement now, at the lovely resort known as Raiford Prison."

I snorted.

We signed off as I turned onto Main Street in Mayfair.

My phone pinged, announcing an incoming text. Becky's name on the Bluetooth screen, under it the words, *You okay?*

I pulled up in front of my house, then sat there for a good two minutes, staring at that screen. How I longed to talk to Becky, share the whole sordid mess with her, have her try to convince me that Susanna Mayfair wasn't a murderer, or at least remind me that I wasn't responsible for her fate.

But despite my anxiety for Susanna, I was loving the way Will was treating me as a partner, sharing the details of the case with me, acknowledging when I gave him a helpful lead.

He'd asked me not to tell Becky and I wasn't going to betray his trust.

I picked up my phone and texted her back.

I'm fine. Sorry life is so crazy. Promise we'll talk soon.

Will's house was still dark when I went to bed. Apparently he hadn't made it back to Mayfair yet.

My sleep was restless, riddled with dreams of karate chops and screaming women. One of them was Becky yelling, "Why haven't you called me?" Finally, as soft light was seeping through the crack between my curtains, I fell into a deep sleep.

And overslept.

I hoped a walk might clear my foggy head so I could focus on my training tasks. Buddy's wagging tail at the sight of his leash announced that he also thought a walk was a splendid idea.

November is one of the best times of the year to live in central Florida. The mornings and evenings are refreshingly cool, the daytime highs in the seventies, usually with low humidity.

I sucked in a deep breath of fresh air as we headed out, turning right toward town. When we neared the bend in the road, I spotted Dexter, a big smile on his face, waving to us from the edge of the vacant field across from the motel. He wore even older clothes than usual, stained dark with sweat, and a red baseball cap on his head.

"Hey, Marcia," he called out.

"Hey, Dexter, what are you up to?" I called back, returning his smile. His carefree air suggested that Edna had still not told him about his mother. I suspected she was waiting to see if Susanna's mind cleared once she was completely weaned from the drugs.

"Will said it was okay to start clearin' some more on this side," Dexter said at a more normal volume as we got closer. "We're gonna expand the motel's parkin' lot, to accommodate the folks comin' to the skatin' rink." He pronounced accommodate carefully, suggesting it was one of this week's additions to his vocabulary.

After my conversation with Sherie the other day, I doubted the skating rink would be happening, at least not by this Christmas. But the entrance to the town would look a lot better with the field cleared.

"You're cutting weeds by hand?" I said. "The backhoe can tear through that much quicker."

"I don't mind." He dropped the tool he'd been using and leaned down to pet Buddy. "Grandpa used to say that sweat was good for the soul."

I felt my smile falter at the mention of his grandfather. How would Dexter feel about the man he'd admired so much, the only father figure he'd ever had, when he found out his grandfather had lied about his mother's suicide and had kept his mother from him all these years?

Buddy was snuffling around in the weeds at Dexter's feet.

"Where's Edna this morning?" I asked. She usually appeared with Bennie and Bo about now.

"She had to go into Ocala early, to get some things. Said I should keep an eye out in case any guests showed up." He gestured toward the motel across the street.

I struggled a bit to keep my expression bland, knowing that Edna wasn't shopping, or at least that wasn't her main reason for going to Ocala.

Meanwhile, Buddy had located whatever smelled so interesting.

I nodded. "Well, I won't keep you from your work."

Dexter's head bobbed in a return nod, then he leaned over. "Look out, boy." He shooed Buddy back and picked up the tool he'd dropped.

I stared at the macheté, my mouth hanging open.

Its curved blade had darkened from age, except for a bright line along the recently sharpened cutting edge. The cracked wooden handle was black at the places where sweaty hands had held it for many years.

Crapola! More like decades. Suddenly my stomach didn't feel so good.

Dexter was now holding the tool upright, the handle poking into the dirt at his feet. Buddy stretched his neck, his nose high in the air, sniffing the spot where the handle met the blade. He whined softly.

I squinted, trying to see what would be so attractive to a dog. "That's a nice macheté," I managed to get out in a reasonably normal voice.

"It's a scythe. People are always gettin' 'em mixed up with machetés. Grandpa used to fuss 'bout that. Said a man should know his tools, and should take good care of 'em, keep 'em sharp and all." There was pride in his voice as he gingerly touched the newly sharpened edge. "This here was Grandpa's. Ain't it in good shape for its age?"

"Yeah." I nodded a little too vigorously. My phone pinged in my pocket. I ignored it.

"Good thing the motel fire didn't reach the old tool shed," Dexter was saying. "I would've really hated to lose Grandpa's tools."

My head bobbed some more. I needed to get out of there. "Well, I'll be seeing you, Dexter."

"Take care, Marcia." He was swinging the scythe before he'd even finished his sentence. It sliced through the thick weeds "like a hot knife through butter," as my mother would say.

I moved away and headed back toward my house. Buddy tilted his head at me, no doubt wondering why I was cutting our walk short.

A low, melodic rumble. I glanced back over my shoulder. Dexter was humming to himself as he mowed down greenery, a serene expression on his face.

My chest ached. Would his cheerful manner survive the revelations that were coming his way?

Once I was out of earshot, I pulled out my phone.

A text from Becky stared up at me. *Call me!*

I ignored it. One hand clutching my queasy stomach, I hit the speed-dial number for Will with the other.

The call went to voicemail. I left a message. "I think Buddy and I found the murder weapon."

CHAPTER NINE

I was ruminating about Dexter's scythe, as I attempted to choke down a late breakfast—it's hard to eat when your throat is closed, but my fickle stomach was now rumbling for food.

What could be so enticing that Buddy would be that persistent about sniffing at the tool?

Was there some dried blood, even after all these years, in the cracks on the handle or under the edge where the metal blade attached to it?

We'd soon find out. Will was on his way to get it and take it to the county crime lab.

The handle was a good three feet long. Long enough that even a slight woman like Susanna could lift it high and bring it down on someone's head with considerable force.

I tried to make myself think about something else. Guilt tightened my chest. I still hadn't called Becky back. I knew for sure I would blurt everything out.

The front door opened. I jumped.

But it was only Will.

"That was quick," I said, amazed that my voice sounded relatively normal.

"When you called, I was checking in with my captain." His voice was grim. "But I was already headed this way from Ocala. The hospital staff said Edna'd been there first thing, but had left. I need to talk to her."

"Can I come?" I was half hoping he would say no. For once my curiosity wasn't dominant. I wouldn't mind putting off getting confirmation about Susanna's role in her husband's death. And if it wasn't her, who else amongst my neighbors would turn out to have been complicit in a murder?

Will was giving me a long, searching look. "Yeah, you know her much better than I do. Watch for signs that she's lying, but *try* to keep your mouth shut."

"Guard the fort," I told Buddy as we walked out the door. Standing in the middle of the living room, he tilted his head in his what's-up look.

My gut twisted. *Wish I knew, boy. Edit that. Wish I didn't have to find out.*

I quickly spotted Edna's gray disheveled head bobbing up and down along the edge of the vacant lot, where Dexter had been working earlier. I raised my hand to point.

"I see her," Will said, his voice low and tense. He wasn't liking this any more than I was.

As we got closer, I was startled by her attire. She wore the old brown sweater over one of Dexter's plaid shirts and baggy sweat pants, with clunky rubber boots on her feet that were obviously too big. Dexter's maybe?

She was madly raking up the dry, dead branches of the bushes and trees that had been dug up by the backhoe before the skeleton's discovery. Nearby a small bonfire was burning.

She hadn't noticed us yet. Dropping the rake, she tore off the brown sweater and threw it with considerable force on top of the fire. It slowly shriveled and then blazed.

Finally our footsteps, crunching on the dry leaves and twigs, registered above the crackle of the fire. She whirled around.

Tears were streaming down her face.

I'd instinctively started to reach out, to gather her into my arms, when she glanced furtively over her shoulder. My gaze followed hers, to the fire.

Light glinted off the raw steel edge of the freshly sharpened scythe lying amongst the burning branches.

Without a word, Will picked up Edna's rake and fished the ancient tool out of the flames. He left it on the grass, its handle smoldering, and dropped the rake beside it.

Taking Edna's elbow, he said, "We need to talk." He gently guided her toward the motel, with me trailing behind.

Sherie Wells suddenly appeared at my side.

I jumped a little. "Uh, good morning." I always tried to remember my manners around Sherie, for fear she'd level that schoolmarm glare of hers at me.

But today her face looked defeated, sagging, an ashen undertone to her brown skin. "I doubt it will be a good one," she said caustically, then closed her lips in a tight line.

We silently mounted the steps of the motel's porch and followed Will and Edna inside.

In the sitting room, Sherie settled beside Edna on the sofa. Will glanced Sherie's way but otherwise didn't acknowledge her presence.

Edna wrinkled her nose and began to push herself to a stand again. "Gonna change first. I stink."

A strong odor of smoke was emanating from her clothes, but Will shook his head.

She sank back with a sigh. She had to know that delaying tactic wouldn't work.

Will sat forward on the edge of the armchair. I was standing off to the side, as instructed, trying to be unobtrusive but watching Edna intently.

He cleared his throat. "Edna, I need–"

She held up her hand, palm out in a stop gesture. "Lemme tell it my own way then."

Will hesitated, then nodded.

"John and me, we were always real close, even growin' up. Our daddy was a self-made man but he taught us to never take nothin' for granted. That and to work hard to improve yer lot in life, to not just sit back and rest on yer laurels."

She laid her hands on her knees, leaning slightly forward, as if it was suddenly too much effort to sit upright. "And he taught us that, in the end, family is everythin'." Her eyes took on that glazed, faraway look. "John wasn't like some older brothers. He always treated me good, let me tag along, made his friends be nice to me even though they thought I was a little nuisance.

"It only seemed natural that I'd tag along on his adventure when he decided to try his hand at runnin' an alligator farm. He bought up all the land 'round here, then deeded a parcel to me for the motel. We had some glory years before it all started fadin' away."

She blinked a few times. "But by then John had married and we had our little Susanna. She was the apple of his eye, and mine too. When she was nine, her mama died." She stopped, took a deep breath. "I felt so guilty. I'd loved John's Mary like a sister, but I was secretly happy to have that little girl all to myself. By that time, it was obvious I was never gonna have a family of my own. Raisin' that little girl, they were the best years of my life. She was so sweet. And then she insisted on going off to school," her face shifted to an angry mask, "and came home married to that man." The last few words were spit out. She grimaced as if they'd left a bad taste in her mouth.

"It was obvious early on that he was a drunk, and John thought he'd been in prison. But we tried to be fair, give the man a chance. Still, neither John nor I could stomach him. Turns out we were right. He was evil through and through."

Sherie reached out and took Edna's hand, gave it a squeeze.

Edna squeezed back as she took another deep breath. "Here's what I know, Will. What I've always known. Thirty-four years ago, that man got drunk as a skunk and beat my niece so badly, the next day she lost the baby she was carryin'. She'd had a sonogram that afternoon and found out it was a little girl. Dexter was gonna have a baby sister. But that man didn't want no more children tyin' him down, so he beat Susie."

Sick to my stomach, I tried to brace myself for what was coming.

"That night, before John even knew she was gonna miscarry, he went after that man. He'd had enough of seein' his only daughter bein' abused." She turned slightly on the sofa to look at Sherie. "And he took Pete Wells with him."

Huh?

"I know," Sherie said softly. "Daddy Wells confessed it all to me when he was dying. I thought it was… No, I *convinced* myself it was the ramblings of an old man's senile brain, but I knew in my heart it wasn't."

Edna's face relaxed some. "Really? I was afraid Susie was making it up."

"Making what up, Edna?" Will asked gently.

Edna turned back to him. "All I knew for sure was that John went to see that man, but I kinda suspected he'd killed him, and when that skeleton showed up… Well, Susie said today that she was startin' to remember things. Things she wasn't sure were real or not. She remembers lookin' through a window and seein' her daddy pick up that scythe and hit her husband over the head with the back of the blade."

Relief whooshed through me. My knees went weak and I grabbed for the back of a nearby chair. Susanna hadn't killed her husband.

"That's pretty much what happened," Sherie said. "Daddy Wells and Mr. Mayfair dragged that drunken scoundrel to the old tool shed. They were gonna beat him up and then tell him to leave and never come back. But he'd sobered up some by then and he was stronger than they'd thought. He fought back pretty hard. He was choking Daddy Wells when Mr. Mayfair hit him."

"Doesn't that make it self-defense?" I blurted out.

Will looked over at me, but there was no censure in his eyes. "Not exactly." He leaned in toward Edna. "I talked to Susanna right after you left. She told me all that, but she'd also remembered something else. She had her first breakdown after she lost the baby, but then her mind cleared and she remembered the confrontation in the shed. She asked her father about it when he came to visit her. She wasn't sure that she hadn't dreamed it all. He said it was true, but that he hadn't meant to kill her husband, just scare him off. He also told her that he and Wells had buried the body back behind the houses of the alligator farm workers, most of whom were gone by then. But she couldn't tell anybody, at least not yet. He was going to put his affairs in order and then turn himself in."

"But he didn't," I said.

Had old man Mayfair intentionally kept his daughter drugged up so she couldn't tell on him? I kept that thought to myself.

Will shook his head. "And then Susanna spiraled into depression again and tried to commit suicide. The doctor at that private hospital at the time, a Lawrence Ames, diagnosed her with chronic severe schizophrenia and depression. His notes in her file indicated that he didn't think she would ever recover."

"The quack," I muttered.

Will nodded. "The forensic accountant found a second trust fund. It was set up to donate five hundred dollars a month to the hospital, as long as Ames and the previous owner, Ellen Brooks, made sure Susanna was getting the best of care."

"Who was the trustee?"

He snorted. "Mayfair's lawyer, who wasn't much younger than him. That was the problem with the whole set-up. Everybody involved was well past sixty at the time. Brooks was already grooming Beckett to take over the place. She died a few years later, as did Dr. Ames and the original trustee. The law firm kept authorizing the payments based on an affidavit Beckett submitted each year, co-signed by the new doc she'd found to help her perpetuate the fraud. It stated that Susanna was still alive, still suffered from incurable mental illness and was being well cared for."

Will looked up at me with an expression in his eyes that I'd only seen once before, the night he'd told me about the young stepson who'd been snatched out of his life when he and his wife had divorced.

Tears pooled in my own eyes. I gritted my teeth.

Will cleared his throat. "The set-up gave Beckett and the doctor ideas. They started soliciting families with mentally-handicapped adult children to bring their kids there, and to set up trust funds for their care after the parents were gone."

I was pretty sure the PC term was *mentally-challenged*, but I wasn't about to correct Will at that moment.

"Do you think that original doctor was after the money," Edna's voice was a little choked, "or was he just incompetent?"

"We may never know that," Will said. "But your brother believed him. I suspect he thought that he *was* sparing you and Dexter more pain by lying about Susanna being dead."

"Dexter. How do I explain all this to him?" Edna buried her face in her hands.

Sherie wrapped both arms around her.

Will stood up, and I moved over beside him. "I think he'll understand," I said gently, "and he'll have his mother back."

"Aunt Edna?"

We all jerked around toward the doorway.

Dexter stood there, his baseball cap in one hand and the sooty scythe in the other. He held it up. "Somehow this got in the fire. I didn't mean to leave it lyin' out." He sounded like a young boy, afraid he was in trouble.

Edna rose. "You didn't. I took it out again, after you'd put it away."

Aunt and great-nephew stared at each other. "You was talkin' about my mama?" Dexter said.

Sherie pushed up off the sofa and herded Will and me toward the door. "Go on in and sit down, boy. Your aunt has some things to talk to you about."

Once out on the porch, I stopped. Will did too.

Sherie's tight jaw and shiny eyes said she was trying not to break down. She went on past us and down the steps without saying a word.

When she was out of earshot, I said, "Are you going to charge Edna or Sherie for not reporting a crime?"

Will shook his head. "They didn't know anything, only suspected, or in Sherie's case, had heard the ramblings of a dying man."

Ramblings about a crime committed by someone who'd already been dead for decades by then.

"That's what I was checking in with my captain about. He said to let it go unless they'd known about the crime at the time." He shook his head again. "You know the saddest thing about this whole mess is, if Mayfair had called the authorities after he hit his son-in-law, he probably wouldn't have gone to jail."

"Really?" My mouth had fallen open a bit. I closed it.

"He had Pete Wells to back him up that he was defending him. And Susanna could have corroborated their stories. Maybe Mayfair and Wells would have been charged with assault, even though technically it was manslaughter, but I doubt they would have done any time. Bart Hill was an ex-con known to have a temper, and Mayfair had a lot of influence back then. At worst, a judge probably would have given him probation."

"Instead, he tried to cover it all up. Maybe to protect Pete Wells. The courts weren't always kind to black men back then."

Will snorted. "Still aren't, all too often."

"Or he was trying to hide it from Susanna initially, afraid she would never forgive him for killing her husband."

Will frowned. "But she already knew, had witnessed the whole thing."

"And Mr. Mayfair ended up dying still thinking he'd driven his daughter incurably insane." My heart ached, for all of them, except maybe the abusive husband who'd lain in a sandy grave for three decades.

Will put his hand on the small of my back. "Come on. Let's go home. I'm taking the rest of the day off."

My phone jangled in my pocket as we walked down the porch steps.

Becky.

Finally I could answer it, no longer afraid of breaking confidences. "Beck, you'll never believe what's been going on around–"

"It's about time you answered your phone! You'll never believe *my* news, *Auntie*."

"Wha'?" I said stupidly, a second before understanding blossomed in my brain.

I turned to Will, a big grin on my face. "Becky's pregnant."

She chuckled in my ear.

EPILOGUE

I squeezed into the only remaining seat at the end of Sherie's navy velveteen sofa, next to her youngest, Sybil. Buddy settled at my feet.

I looked around the crowded room. *Thank you, Mom.*

My mother had been remarkably understanding when I'd told her I couldn't make it home for Christmas. Granted I'd given several hard-to-refute excuses, um, I mean, reasons. Finances were tight—always true. I couldn't interrupt Rocky's and Josie's training. And the one that I'm sure sealed the deal—I wanted to spend the holiday with Will, our first Christmas together, and he was too new at the Marion County Sheriff's Department to get enough time off for traveling.

The fourth reason, which I hadn't told her, was that I really wanted to spend Christmas with my Mayfair "family." Old wounds had been ripped open and rubbed raw, and I wanted to do what I could to comfort and support those affected.

"So, how's it going, Syb?" I asked the young woman next to me.

She flashed me a big grin. "Great. One more semester and I'm a nurse!"

"Awesome," I said, returning the grin. Sybil had recently moved in with friends in Ocala, to be closer to school and her part-time job. Sherie was now a true empty-nester.

I surveyed the crowd again. A dozen adults sitting on every type of seat imaginable, including a kitchen stool, smiled and chatted with those around them. Most were drinking sweet tea or eggnog, nonalcoholic—Sherie did not allow liquor in her house. Six or seven young heads, kids from two to ten, bobbed about between the adults. Two teens sat on the floor in a corner, playing handheld video games. And one baby was being dangled on her father's knee.

"Are these all relatives?" I asked.

"Mostly," Sybil said. "Some are 'adopted,'" she made air quotes, "like you." The wide grin again.

We both turned and looked at the only other white faces in the crowd. Edna Mayfair was ensconced in Sherie's recliner next to a brand new, flat-screen TV, Sherie's gift from her kids.

Today, Edna wore a muumuu with white and red poinsettias on an emerald green background. A cheap black sweater had replaced the old brown one that had been her brother's. With a jolt, I realized the muumuus were all the same shape, or rather shapeless in the same way. Edna made them herself.

No one would ever guess that she was an heiress.

Dexter sat next to his aunt, on a straight-backed chair from the kitchen. A contented smile on his face, his gaze moved from one jovial cluster to another, his head nodding to the beat of the Christmas music playing softly in the background.

Most of the folks here were staying at the motel, free of charge, since Edna had rooms to spare. The Christmas extravaganza had never happened. With all the upheaval in November, there had been insufficient time and energy, physical or emotional, to devote to it.

But our newly formed Chamber of Commerce was already focusing on next Christmas. It scared me some that they had a whole year to plan for it.

Sherie walked into the middle of the room and clapped her hands. The conversations died. "Each child can pick one present to open tonight. The rest, you will have to wait until tomorrow morning to open."

A mad scramble ensued as children attempted to find the gifts with their names on them, then rattled and prodded, trying to figure out if it was something fun or just boring clothes.

The front door, near my end of the sofa, swung open. Will stepped into the doorway, backlit by the setting sun. "Merry Christmas, everyone," he called out.

All adult heads swung his way. The kids were too busy ripping paper off their chosen gifts.

"I have a Christmas Eve present for a couple of folks here," he announced. "Somebody was ready to come home from the rehab center sooner than expected." He stepped to one side.

Susanna Mayfair took a small step forward and smiled shyly at the crowd.

The room exploded with applause.

Susanna blushed. She wore a red silk blouse and black jeans and had filled out some since I'd last seen her, looking pale and stark and acting crazy in that hospital room.

Edna was struggling to get out of the recliner. "Help me, Dexter."

But her nephew hadn't heard her in the hubbub. He jumped up himself, his eyes glued to his mother's face.

I was relieved to see his gleeful expression. Edna had taken him to the hospital a few times to see Susanna, and then later to the rehabilitation center where they'd continued to wean her from the drug cocktail she'd been on. Edna had shared with me that mother and son had been a bit awkward with each other.

I could only imagine what it must be like to meet a full-grown son whom you hadn't seen since he was four. Or to be a grown man meeting the mother you barely remembered and had long since thought was dead.

Dexter rushed across the room, arms outspread. “Mama, you’re home.”

Susanna beamed and tentatively returned his hug.

Sherie greeted her childhood friend with tears streaming down her face. Then Edna ushered Susanna to the recliner and Dexter went off to get another chair from the kitchen.

As the chatter in the room resumed, Will perched on the over-stuffed arm of the sofa and took my hand. He leaned close to my ear and whispered, “She wanted to surprise them.”

I grinned up at him. “I think she succeeded.”

“Her new diagnosis is drug-induced dementia, in remission, and major depressive disorder. She’s on a mild antidepressant.”

I nodded. That sounded much more appropriate than chronic schizophrenia.

When Sherie had fetched glasses for Susanna and Will and had made the rounds, refreshing everyone’s tea or eggnog, I stood. Taking a step forward, I clinked my spoon against my iced-tea glass. Buddy rose and stood at my knee.

Everyone quieted—well, the kids were still squealing some over their presents, but I could make myself heard above them. “Since I can’t be with my mom this year, I’d like to bring a little bit of her here to us. I’d like to share her favorite Christmas toast with you all.”

The adults quieted even more, some of them hushing the kids.

One hand on Buddy’s head, I raised my glass in the air with the other. “In the words of Tiny Tim, ‘God bless us, one and all.’”

Sherie and Will chuckled. Edna and Dexter looked vaguely confused, but they lifted their glasses and then took a sip of tea.

Will raised his glass. “To many happy Christmases to come.”

“Here, here,” several people cheered.

Sherie stepped over to me and slid an arm around my waist. We both watched Edna and Susanna, heads tilted together, talking and smiling.

Buddy shifted under my hand. I scratched behind his ear.

Sherie leaned in closer to me. "Thank the good Lord the ghost of Christmas past has finally been put to rest," she whispered.

Not trusting my voice, I just nodded.

AUTHOR NOTES

If you enjoyed this book, please take a moment to leave a short review on the book retailer's site where you downloaded it (and/or other online book retailers). Reviews help with sales, and sales keep the series going! You can find the links for these retailers at the *misterio press* bookstore at https://misteriopress.com.

Also, you may want to go to https://kassandralamb.com to sign up for my newsletter and get updates on new releases, giveaways and sales (and you get a free e-copy of a novella for signing up). I only send out newsletters when I truly have news and you can unsubscribe at any time.

We at *misterio press* pride ourselves on providing our readers with top-quality reads. All of our books are proofread multiple times by several pairs of eyes, but proofreaders are human. If you found errors in this book, please email me at lambkassandra3@gmail.com so the errors can be corrected. Thank you!

Quoting Tiny Tim was *my* mother's favorite toast at Christmas dinner.

She was blessed with a long and mostly happy life. I still miss her, especially at Christmas time.

A big thank you to the usual partners in crime: Vinnie Hansen, one of our *misterio press* authors who critiqued and proofread this story early on; Shannon Esposito, my partner at *misterio*, who always props me up when my will to write sags; my wonderful daughter-in-law, romance writer G.G. Andrew, who read and offered her usual dead-on feedback; and my wonderful husband who is my final proofreader.

Although Sunny, Sunshine and Palms are part of the names of several retirement centers in Florida, there is no Sunny Palms Retirement Center in Marion County, nor in the rest of the state, to the best of my knowledge. Nor is there a nursing agency, Belleview Nightingales, that I know of. If there is, the names used in this story are purely coincidental.

I can't recall what planted the seed for this story, but as I got into it, I really loved exploring the unfolding backstory of the Mayfair clan.

But this was a Christmas story. I needed a happy ending. So I decided to bring Dexter's mother back to life.

While I doubt there is anyone being held in an institution for fraudulent monetary gain—that is a figment of my twisted imagination—there was a time when schizophrenia was very much an over-diagnosed disorder.

First let me clarify that schizophrenia is NOT split personalities. That is a completely different disorder, now called dissociative identity disorder.

Schizophrenia is a serious thought disorder, caused by genetics, chemical imbalances and possibly structural changes to the brain that occur prenatally. Schizophrenics can suffer from delusions, hallucinations, seriously disordered thinking, incoherent speech, etc. But severely depressed people can also exhibit delusions and sometimes even hallucinations. And a few other disorders have some symptoms in common with schizophrenia.

Those of us who were in the mental health field in the 1980s and 90s heard many a horror story about patients who'd had the schizophrenia label slapped on them, in previous decades, for everything from postpartum depression to autism to teenage rebellion. The stigma of that diagnosis would then haunt the person for the rest of their lives.

Fortunately today, there have been significant improvements in diagnostic criteria and in patients' rights, so we rarely see this diagnosis wrongly applied now.

But when I was looking for a way that Dexter's mother might have been kept away from her family in Mayfair for all these years, a private mental hospital that flew under the bureaucratic radar seemed like the ticket.

I hope you enjoyed this story. I plan on writing similar stories for other holidays, such as July 4th (*A Star-Spangled Mayfair*) and Halloween (no title yet). In them, the focus will be more on happenings in Mayfair rather than Marcia's work with veterans and her dogs.

Stay tuned for the next of those stories about an American Staffordshire Terrier, a sometimes misunderstood and maligned breed, who is paired up with a slightly paranoid former Navy seaman who believes he is misunderstood and maligned.

Here's a brief synopsis of ***Patches in the Rye, A Marcia Banks and Buddy Mystery, Book 5*** and an excerpt:

Nothing about her new client is what service dog trainer Marcia Banks expected—from the posh house that says family money to his paranoid preoccupation with his sister's love life—but when he dangles a thousand-dollar retainer under her nose, she can't resist playing private detective.

In between training sessions, Marcia digs into the sister's boyfriend's sketchy past. But the deeper she digs, the more questions arise. How is a disastrous fraternity party five years ago linked to blackmail, prostitutes, and murder today? And who's driving the black SUV that keeps trying to turn Marcia and her dog Buddy into roadkill?

She can't let it go, not when there are innocents at risk who are depending on her to find the truth. But the deepest, darkest truth is the one she wishes she never uncovered.

Patches in the Rye

CHAPTER ONE

I stared up at the large white house, a mini-mansion really, and swallowed. Buddy and I climbed the steps to the broad, pillared porch. The buzz of an electric trimmer, wielded by a gardener manicuring an already pristine lawn, reminded me of a swarm of angry bees.

The noise covered the sound of the doorbell as I pushed the button beside the door. After a moment, I debated if I should knock.

Not yet. If the former Navy Chief Petty Officer actually answered his own door—with a place like this, he might have servants—it would probably take him awhile. I didn't want to make him feel rushed.

I was daydreaming, trying to jive the non-commissioned officer rank with the fancy house, when the door flew open, banging against the inside wall so hard the glass panels around its frame rattled.

And suddenly I was staring at a substantial amount of cleavage, tucked into a snug pink top. Long legs in tight jeans were already moving before the owner of the cleavage seemed to register that someone was standing in her way. She veered slightly to the side, but still came close to bowling Buddy and me over.

I caught a glimpse of her face as she barreled past us, mumbling, “Sorry.” Long, straight blonde hair, red-rimmed blue eyes, tear tracks on fair cheeks, an overall impression of beauty and youth.

I turned to stare after the teenager, my mind conjuring up a sordid explanation for why she was running away from my client.

“Sorry.” This time, the word was delivered in a rumbling male voice coming from the open doorway behind me.

I turned back with a plastered-on smile, then had to lower my gaze to make eye contact with the man in the doorway. “Roger Campbell?”

“Yeah,” he said. He wore a blond buzz cut, a faded Navy tee shirt and a dark green throw over his legs. “And you just met my sister, Alexis.”

Watch those assumptions. My mother’s voice. Even inside my head, she was annoyingly right most of the time.

Campbell whirled his wheelchair around. “Come on in.”

He led Buddy and me down a long wide hallway, dim rooms on either side, with blinds mostly closed to protect dusty antiques from the Florida sun. A formal parlor, a dining room, and a library with shelves and shelves of books that made me salivate.

It was on my bucket list to someday own a home big enough for a separate library.

The hallway opened into a sparsely furnished area, a great room. No rugs or coffee tables cluttered the space. A tan leather sofa, matching loveseat, end table, and overstuffed armchair lined half the perimeter of the expanse of hardwood floor. A large, flat screen TV hung on the wall opposite the sofa.

The room would have been attractive—spacious with a lived-in air—if the dark wooden blinds covering the many windows weren't completely closed. Instead it resembled a giant cave, with only a few scattered lamps casting a feeble glow.

In one corner, a round oak table was surrounded by three chairs, with an open gap where one would expect a fourth to be. Roger's place at the table, no doubt.

That was confirmed when he maneuvered his wheelchair around in that spot until he was sideways to the table. He gestured toward the nearby loveseat.

A beer bottle sat on a placemat at his elbow. He nodded toward the bottle. "Want one?"

Another fake smile. "No, thank you." I perched on the edge of the loveseat and signaled for Buddy to lay down at my feet.

"I'm Marcia Banks." I'm sure he'd been given my name, but it seemed polite to introduce myself. "And this is Buddy, my mentor dog. He'll be helping to train whatever dog we pick for you."

This preliminary visit was a new addition to the process that Mattie Jones, the director of the agency I trained for, hoped would help the trainers assess what kind of dog would be most appropriate for new clients.

"Do you have any preferences regarding breed?" I asked to get things rolling.

Campbell shook his head without meeting my gaze. His mind seemed to be elsewhere.

"Can you tell me how you sustained your injuries?"

Suddenly his blue eyes, darker than his sister's, were focused on me—two mini laser beams. "Can't. Classified," he said brusquely.

I nodded, even though I knew that was probably horse hockey. If the operation where he'd been injured was truly secret, he would have given me the cover story, not said out loud that it was classified.

I caught myself reaching back to twirl my long ponytail of auburn hair around my fingers, a sure sign that I was more nervous than usual. Dropping my hand back into my lap, I said, "I'm not being nosy. I need to assess what kinds of things are triggers for you, what might set off a flashback, such as loud noises."

I'd be training his service dog to help with physical needs, such as picking up objects dropped on the floor, but our dogs were mainly trained to help veterans cope with PTSD and other psychological symptoms related to their service.

He gave me a grim smile. "I was on an aircraft carrier. I'm used to loud noises."

I opted to give up on this tooth-pulling process. We had a waiver of confidentiality from him and I suspected Mattie had a detailed report on his symptoms by now, although it wouldn't say much about the operation in which they were sustained, even if it wasn't classified.

I'd come back to that question another time, if necessary.

I launched into my spiel about how the process would proceed, that I'd pick a dog and bring it over to make sure they hit it off, before starting the expensive training process. Then it would be several months before he heard from me again, at which point I'd set up some times to meet and teach him how to work with the dog.

He was barely listening, looking at the door periodically and glancing at his watch.

Sheez, what's with this guy? snarky me said inside my head. I hid a proud smile. Ms. Snark, as I thought of that part of myself, was getting so much better at not blurting out her thoughts.

I went back to my spiel. Campbell glanced at his watch again.

I tried to mentally slap a hand over Ms. Snark's mouth, but I was too late. "Am I keeping you from something more important?"

He had the good grace to blush a little. "Sorry. I guess I'm preoccupied."

Duh, Ms. Snark said internally.

He used his elbows to push against the arms of the chair and sit up straighter. "Mar-see-a." He emphasized each syllable of my name. "Where'd you get that name?"

From my parents, like most people, Ms. Snark said inside. I imagined putting duct tape over her mouth.

I dug deep for another fake smile. "My mother thought that was more unique and melodic than Marsha, even though it's spelled M-a-r-c-i-a."

He nodded, and I went on, describing some of the things I would train his dog to do.

Again he was distracted, staring at the opening to the hallway. From where I was sitting, I could see an edge of the front door's frame. He would have a full frontal view.

I cleared my throat.

His head swiveled back toward me. Again he shoved himself more upright. "Sorry. I'm just worried about my sister."

This time my small smile was more genuine. "I gathered that."

I have a masters degree in counseling psychology and, although I've never been in practice, I use the skills I'd learned to get clients talking. This time, however, I wasn't sure I wanted to know what drama was behind his sister's precipitous exit.

"It's only me and Alexis now…"

Crapola. Apparently, he was going to tell me anyway.

"Both our parents are dead." His voice was hoarse. "And I think I'm losing her."

I stifled a sigh. "How so?"

"She's dating this guy who's too old for her, and he's got a criminal record. We used to be really close, but now we fight most of the time, usually about him."

"How old is he?"

"Twenty-six."

A year younger than Roger Campbell himself, if I was remembering his age correctly. But still way too old for Alexis. "How old is your sister?"

"Twenty."

Wow. I'd have guessed sixteen or seventeen. Did her youthful appearance make her brother more protective of her?

My older brother had never been particularly protective. When we were kids, he was the one I most often needed protection *from*. But we got along fine now. When Ben's oldest picked on his younger brother at family gatherings, I'd roll my eyes at Ben and smirk. If no one was watching, he'd stick out his tongue at me and then grin.

Elbows on the chair arms, Campbell leaned forward a little. "Do you happen to know any private investigators? I want somebody to look into this guy."

The abrupt change of subject surprised me, the word *investigator* making my heart beat faster.

"I'm sure there's more dirt there." He grimaced. "Besides the sealed juvenile record I was able to find." He looked at me with a hopeful expression. "I'll pay good."

The corner of my brain that constantly worries about money perked up. An image of my past due electric bill flashed into my mind's eye.

I tried to tamp down both my excitement and my avarice. *I am* not *a private investigator,* I told myself.

"No, I don't know anybody, but my boyfriend might." I kind of hated that term for an almost forty-year-old divorced cop, but for lack of a better word. "He's a police detective."

Campbell frowned but then shifted his expression to a smile. "Would you ask him?"

"Sure."

"That would be great." The smile was still there, but his eyes didn't look all that happy.

He paid closer attention to the rest of my spiel after that.

"I'll be in touch, once I've found a suitable dog." I pushed myself to a stand and Buddy rose too, giving his body a small shake.

"Don't get up. We can find our…" Heat crept up my cheeks as I realized my blunder.

The ends of Campbell's mouth quirked up and his eyes sparkled with amusement. It was the first genuine expression he'd exhibited. "I'll let you see yourself out."

Once on the porch, I paused and lifted my face to the Florida sun, already intense even in early March. Its warmth chased away the slight chill running through my body.

"Happy anniversary," Becky trilled in my ear when I answered her call.

"Thanks." My tone was less than enthusiastic.

"So what are you two doing to celebrate one year of dating?"

"I'm eating a poptart and reading a client's file. Will's chasing bad guys."

"Oh sweetie." Becky's voice deflated.

"Yeah, well. Goes with the territory." Will had recently transitioned from the sheriff of a small rural county to a detective in a much larger county's sheriff's department, primarily so that he could move closer to me. He considered it a lateral career shift and was happy to be solving crimes again rather than attending eternal meetings with county commissioners.

But it had its downside. He no longer controlled his own schedule. So our plans to celebrate the anniversary of our first date had gone by the wayside when a string of armed bank robberies threatened to put Marion County on the map, and not in a good way.

Tired of my pity party, I changed the subject. "How's little Buster or Betty Boop doing?"

"Behaving his/herself lately. No more morning sickness."

I brightened a bit. Some good news tonight at least. "That's great."

"So can you meet me for lunch tomorrow?" Becky asked.

I slumped in my kitchen chair again. "Can't. I'm dog hunting."

"You still gotta eat." Her voice sounded borderline desperate.

"I'll probably be running all over central Florida, and once I get this dog rolling with their training, I'll need to start another one." Normally I liked to have one dog about halfway through their training before starting another, but multiple recent events had disrupted that pattern, and had left my bank account on life support.

"I could go with you," Becky was saying. "I'm dying of boredom down here."

I got that. It was one of the many reasons I'd resisted moving in with Will when he was still sheriff of Collins County, the position Becky's husband Andy now held.

"You know that's a bad idea, Beck. You'll come home with a half dozen puppies."

A deep sigh. "Yeah. I've got no willpower where cute is concerned." A pause. "So when can you get together?" The whine in her voice was unmistakable, and out of character.

"Soon, I hope. I–" A mind-boggling idea blossomed in my brain, stalling my tongue. I knew instantly that it had been percolating ever since Roger Campbell had asked me about private investigators.

And I also knew that pretty much everyone who cared about me would hate it.

"You still there?" Becky said in my ear.

The doorbell rang before I could answer her. I jumped up and headed for the living room. "Hang on. Someone's at my door."

I peeked out my front window. A stranger in jeans and a tee shirt stood on my porch. Shafts of bright light from the setting sun lit up the cleared field across from my house. One sunbeam spotlighted the giant bouquet of multi-colored roses in the man's hands. A green panel truck, parked at the curb behind my car, sported *Belleview Florist* on its side in pink frilly letters.

"Will sent me flowers," I told Becky as I threw open the door.

The guy said my name, mispronouncing it as Marsha, of course. I nodded, too pleased by the sight of the roses to bother correcting him. Grinning, he relinquished the bouquet and trotted to his truck.

"Is there a card?" Becky asked.

"Yeah." I read it silently as I stepped back inside the house, then found it difficult to get the words past a lump in my throat. "He says he'll make it up to me."

"Why so glum?" Becky asked.

"Not glum, guilty." I sighed. "I'm the reason he took this job, remember? I should be making it up to *him*."

Becky spent the next five minutes trying to convince me that Will had made his own choices regarding his career and I had nothing to feel guilty about. It was a nice try, but I wasn't buying it. I knew darn well that in the meeting-each-other-halfway aspect of relationships, he'd gone seventy-five percent of the way and I was barely at twenty.

And if I implemented my new bright idea for making more money, I'd be backsliding to about ten percent. I glanced at the pile of unpaid bills on my coffee table and grimaced.

CHAPTER TWO

With morning coffee close at hand, I sat at my kitchen table perusing Mattie's list of donated dogs currently being fostered by agency staff members or volunteers. All the dogs were too young and still being trained in the basics by their foster parents.

I started calling the rescue shelters in central Florida. Mattie has an understanding with many of them allowing us to take a dog on a trial basis. But none of them had a dog that met our criteria.

I remembered the young woman I'd met at the Buckland County shelter last summer. Buckland Beach was on the east coast, two hours away, but I was getting desperate. I called their number while I tried without success to recall the woman's name.

I was in luck. The chirpy young woman who answered the phone said that yes, *she* remembered me. "Jake Black's friend. He's been in several times, since… all that happened. He and his wife now foster some of our kittens."

Jake Black was a former client—not really a friend *per se*—and "all that" referred to the two times his service dog Felix had been sent to the Buckland shelter when Jake and his wife were arrested, first for robbery and then for murder. One of those times Buddy had been in the house with Felix and had also been hauled away. I never wanted to relive that horrible Saturday afternoon when I was desperate to get to the shelter before it closed, and would be closed for the next two days. I'd felt like child protective services had taken my kid away from me.

"I'm sorry but I can't seem to remember your name," I said.

She giggled. "I'm not sure I ever gave it to you. Stephie, um, Stephanie Wilson."

My brain conjured up an image of her young face, smooth and round, with big brown eyes and a halo of frizzy dark hair.

I told Stephie I was searching for a dog for a new client and gave her the criteria.

She thought for a moment. "I may have just the guy for you, a Heinz 57. But he's not quite that tall."

A Heinz 57, a mix of many breeds. Not a bad thing. Mutts were often healthier than dogs who came from more limited gene pools.

"How much shorter than twenty-four inches?"

A beat of silence. "Maybe two, but he's muscular, weighs about sixty pounds. And he's really well-mannered and eager to please."

I considered the fact that Roger Campbell was in a wheelchair. His file had revealed that he'd fallen off of an airplane wing during a maintenance inspection and landed hard on the aircraft carrier's deck, sustaining "severe and most likely permanent injury to his spinal cord."

You can bet Ms. Snark had some things to say about that *classified* mission! But the ignoble way he'd sustained the injury didn't make him less of a hero to me. Anyone who was willing to serve our country in the military is a hero in my book.

What *had* bothered me a little was his general discharge, under honorable conditions—a discharge that sometimes, but not always, meant the recipient was a troublemaker.

"You still there?" Stephie said in my ear.

"Yes." Since Roger Campbell would be wheelchair-bound for the foreseeable future, a shorter dog should work fine. Might even be better. "Any aggressive behaviors or fears?" I asked.

"None that we've seen. And he knows all the basic commands—come, sit, lie down, stay."

"Can you hold him for me? Until I can get over to the coast."

"Um, I guess so. For a few hours."

"I'll be there in two."

I figured the dog was a long shot, but Mattie would reimburse me for the gas. And I'd remembered Stephie had expressed an interest in learning to be a trainer.

My bright idea was beginning to solidify into a half-baked plan. If I had help with the training, I'd have time to explore a possible new career.

Two hours later, I was eyeing the dog dubiously. "Looks like he's got some pit bull in him."

"We don't think so." Stephie was trying to hand me his leash, which I was passively resisting by keeping my hands at my sides.

"Our vet said he's probably half American Staffordshire Terrier, with a conglomeration of a few other breeds thrown in. Amstaffs are cousins of pit bulls, but they have somewhat different personalities."

I was still skeptical. "Aren't they dog-aggressive, like pits can be?" A dog that reacted much to other animals, either overly friendly or aggressive, would be too easily distracted to be a good service dog.

"Sometimes," Stephie said, "but this guy's fine with other dogs."

I arched an eyebrow at her.

"Come on. I'll show you." She turned and led the dog away. Short of being rude, a mortal sin according to my mother, I had to follow.

Stephie opened the gate to a fenced enclosure. She turned the mutt loose in it. He bounded away and started sniffing clumps of grass. "I'll be right back."

I was getting to know the boy—he was adorable, white with tan patches and an intelligent face—when Stephie returned with two other dogs in tow. Both were smaller than the Amstaff, one some kind of terrier mix half his size and the other a Chihuahua, who was snapping at the terrier. Stephie was struggling to keep them apart.

I went over and helped her with the gate. Once inside, she let the dogs off their leashes. The Chihuahua went after the Amstaff, stopping just shy of his nose and putting on her best snarling and snapping routine. The terrier stood by the gate, barking, hair standing up on his back.

The Amstaff cocked his head at both of them. They could have been inanimate objects that someone had wound up and set loose. Indeed, he might have reacted more to such objects, as toys. These nuisance dogs he ignored.

"What's his name?" I tried to sound gruff, like I was still resisting the idea.

Stephie grinned. She knew I was hooked. "We've been calling him Patches."

It suited him. And it was a good name for a service dog—short and simple, easy to call out quickly to get his attention.

I turned to the young woman. "Did you ever call Mattie Jones about becoming a trainer?"

Her cheeks turned a light shade of pink. "Yeah. She said I'd be a good candidate, but then I got busy with the fall semester and never followed up. I go to Buckland Community College."

"Will you have time for training if I ask you to train under me?"

Her blush deepened and she nodded her head, dark curls bouncing. "I'll make time."

"I'm two hours away."

That gave her pause, but only for a moment. "I can probably get over there for a good chunk of time at least three days a week."

"That should work. I need to take the dog on a two-week trial basis, see if he's going to work out."

"I think the adoption director will go along with that."

"I'll clear the training with Mattie," I said.

We both nodded and grinned at each other.

Will made it home for a late dinner. Fully aware of my limited culinary skills, he'd stopped for pizza along the way.

Now, by "home" I mean my house, even though it technically wasn't Will's home. When I'd resisted living together—the next logical step in our relationship—he had bought the fixer-upper next door to me and made the job change to the Marion County Sheriff's Department.

Every time I thought about those changes he'd willingly made, my chest felt light and warm even as my gut twisted a little with guilt.

I didn't deserve a guy who would go to such lengths to be close to me when I wasn't willing to commit past breakfast the next morning.

So now we did this odd combination of living together but not, often eating together and sleeping together, usually in my kitchen and bedroom respectively.

I didn't feel particularly guilty about our "conjugal visits" as Becky laughingly calls them. We'd both been married and divorced, hardly blushing virgins. Although I still hadn't told my rather old-fashioned mother, a pastor's widow, that Will lived right next door now. With fingers crossed behind my back, I'd told her he'd moved closer to me and our relationship was going well. Which was the truth, just not the absolute whole truth.

Between bites of pizza and trying to act nonchalant, I asked him about good private investigators in the area.

"Why do you need a P.I.?"

"It's for a client."

His blue eyes sparkled and a grin stretched across his rugged face. "Phew! You had me worried for a minute."

My stomach clenched. I knew Will was *not* going to like my half-baked plan. Would it be the final straw for him?

I was five-seven, curvier than was fashionable, with freckles on what I thought was a rather plain face. My only really good feature was my long dark hair with its red highlights. I seriously doubted I'd ever attract another man like Will.

But… I desperately needed money. Events beyond my control last summer had both cost me money and slowed down my training schedule, and the occasional online psych classes I'd been teaching for a local college had disappeared when they'd hired more full-time faculty.

Plus a year ago, I'd totaled my car in a close encounter with a palm tree. Again, not my fault. At the time, a guy was standing behind the car about to blast me with a shotgun.

Now I had car payments and higher insurance premiums. The insurance company was skeptical of the shotgun story.

I held my breath, as Will thought for a moment. If he did know a good P.I. maybe that would be a sign that I shouldn't do this. At any rate, I was trying not to tell him what I was contemplating, until it was real.

Dropping a thin strip of pizza crust on his paper plate, he put his hands behind his neck, elbows sticking out, and stretched to loosen tight muscles.

I almost swooned as said muscles rippled in his tanned arms.

Leaning his chair on its back legs, he finally said, "Can't think of any. Know a few bad ones. I'm sure there are some good ones around, but I haven't crossed paths with them yet."

Keeping my gaze on my plate, I asked, "Um, how does one go about getting a background check on someone, and how much does it cost?"

I felt more than saw Will jerk a bit in his chair across from me. The chair's front legs hit the floor with a thud.

A beat of silence. I was afraid to look at his face.

"There are online companies that do them." His voice was neutral, maybe too neutral. "For one worth having, they run about fifty to a hundred. Why do you need a background check on someone?"

"A client seems a little weird."

"Same client?"

Sure, I'd call Campbell "a little weird."

"Yes."

"I could run it for you." He sounded more normal. "But don't tell anyone about it, and it would be illegal for you to openly use the info against the person."

I was a tad surprised by the offer. Usually Will was pretty by the book.

I crossed my fingers under the table. "That's okay. Since I've already told you it's a client, I really can't say his name now. Confidentiality and all that." Actually, I didn't even know the name of the young man my client wanted investigated.

I made myself meet his gaze and managed a smile. "If I find something bad, Mattie will probably reimburse me. And if I don't, it will be worth it. I'll feel more comfortable working with him."

He returned my smile. "Good to see you being so careful."

I felt like a worm, until I decided that maybe I should run a background check on Campbell after all, as well as his sister's boyfriend.

I relaxed. Now I *was* telling the truth. Again, not the whole truth, but hey….

And my plan felt more like two-thirds baked now. All I had to do was get Roger Campbell to go along with it.

The next morning, I knocked on the Campbells' door, then stepped well back, gesturing for Buddy to follow suit. He cocked his head, giving me his patented what's-up expression.

"To avoid flying sisters," I whispered to him.

I glanced at my car, parked at the curb in the shade of a live oak tree. I'd left Patches in the backseat until I could assess the situation with Roger Campbell.

He answered the door and gave me a pleasant enough smile. "Ms. Banks, come on in."

"Please, call me Marcia." I stepped over the threshold and looked around. The house was quiet. Maybe his sister wasn't home.

His smile widened. "Okay, and I'm Roger."

"Are you ready to meet your potential service dog?" I said with an exaggerated smile of my own.

"Sure." His tone wasn't completely enthusiastic, but it wasn't hesitant either.

Even after I'd shelled out fifty bucks for an online background check of this guy, I still had reservations about him. Why, I couldn't quite pinpoint. The only thing I'd come up with was that he'd made no move to interact with Buddy the last time we'd been here.

It was as if the dog didn't even exist, which pegged Campbell as not much of a dog person. But then again, he had been distracted.

He didn't have to love dogs, but he had to at least like them. So I'd designed a little test. I gave Buddy the release signal—hands crossed at the wrists, then opened wide—a gesture one was not likely to make accidentally.

"I'm going to leave Buddy here while I get Patches. I've released him from duty so it's okay to pet him." Buddy gave a tentative wag of his big black tail.

I paused for a moment before turning back toward the front door.

Roger Campbell patted the lap throw over his thighs. "Come here, boy."

Buddy trotted over, and Roger held out his hand in a loose fist for the dog to sniff it. Then he patted Buddy's shoulder, before moving his hand up to scratch behind an ear.

Buddy's tail was waving like a conductor's baton.

Okay, enough of a dog person to know how to interact with a strange dog. Most of my tense muscles relaxed.

I went out to my car to fetch Patches.

After dog and man had gotten to know each other—with some sniffing and ear scratching—I gestured for both Patches and Buddy to lie down, my hand parallel to the floor and moving straight down. I added a verbal, "Lie down," for Patches's benefit. He hadn't quite made the connection yet to the hand gesture.

"So what do you think?" I asked.

Roger smiled at the dog, a good sign. "He's a handsome fellow, and he seems pretty bright."

"I think he's going to work out fine. I'll work on some preliminary tasks this week and get a better feel for how trainable he is."

He gave one slight nod of his head, then asked, "Did you find out about a private investigator?"

I shifted mentally to that subject. "My boyfriend didn't know anyone he was willing to recommend."

Roger's gaze dropped to his knees. His face slowly turned red. Suddenly, he smacked the arms of the wheelchair with his hands, making me jump.

Buddy looked up at me, worry in his eyes. I shook my head slightly.

Roger started cursing a blue streak.

I cringed a little inside. I'm no prude, mind you, but my mother was really strict about swearing. My friends know it makes me uncomfortable and try to resist cussing around me.

Thus the phrase, "cussed like a sailor." For once, I was grateful for Ms. Snark's commentary. I relaxed some.

Until he smacked the chair arms again. "A man needs to be able to protect his family."

I took a deep breath, debating now if I should mention my two-thirds baked plan. Something about this whole scenario felt off.

But Roger went there first. Dark blue eyes boring into mine, he said, "I heard you're a pretty decent detective yourself."

I feigned surprise. Actually, that wasn't too hard since I *was* somewhat surprised by his statement. "Where'd you hear that?"

"Retired vets' grapevine. I heard you helped Jake Black out of a fix last summer."

I gave a slight nod and let out a slow breath, thankful that he hadn't heard about my first attempt at detecting, which hadn't ended nearly as well.

"Could you check out my sister's boyfriend for me?"

I gave a small self-deprecating shrug, which I'd practiced several times in the mirror that morning. "I guess I could try."

Roger wheeled over to a small desk in a corner of the room. He pulled a checkbook over in front of him. "How's a thousand dollars as a retainer sound?"

Like a bunch of overdue bills getting paid off, Ms. Snark commented internally. I reminded her that I was going to keep the money in my savings account until I was sure I'd earned it.

"That's fine," I said out loud, trying to keep my expression serious. Excitement bubbled in my chest. "I'll need more information."

Thirty minutes later, I left the Campbell residence with a dog to train, a check to deposit and a decision to make about how and where to start in my role as private eye.

My other quandary was how to explain to Will that I was once again sticking my toe in the detecting pool, this time quite intentionally, and that I might be considering—not a career change *per se*, but a career addition.

ABOUT THE AUTHOR

Kassandra Lamb has never been able to decide which she loves more, psychology or writing. In college, she realized that writers need a day job in order to eat, so she studied psychology. After a career as a psychotherapist and college professor, she is now retired and can pursue her passion for writing. She spends most of her time in an alternate universe with her characters. The portal to this universe, aka her computer, is located in Florida, where her husband and dog catch occasional glimpses of her. She and her husband spend part of each summer in her native Maryland, where her Kate Huntington series is based.

Kass is currently working on Book 10 of the Kate Huntington mystery series and Book 7 of the Marcia Banks and Buddy cozy mysteries. She also has four novellas out in the Kate on Vacation series (lighter reads along the lines of cozy mysteries but with the same main characters as the Kate Huntington series).

To read and see more about Kassandra and her characters you can go to https://kassandralamb.com. Be sure to sign up for the newsletter there to get a heads up about new releases, plus special offers and bonuses for subscribers. (New subscribers get a free e-copy of a novella.)

Kass's e-mail is lambkassandra3@gmail.com and she loves hearing from readers! She's also on Facebook and hangs out some on Twitter @KassandraLamb. She blogs about psychological topics and other random things at https://misteriopress.com.

Please check out these other great *misterio press* series:

Karma's A Bitch: The Pet Psychic Mysteries
by Shannon Esposito

Multiple Motives: The Kate Huntington Mysteries
by Kassandra Lamb

Maui Widow Waltz: The Islands of Aloha Mysteries
by JoAnn Bassett

The Metaphysical Detective: The Riga Hayworth Paranormal Mysteries
by Kirsten Weiss

Dangerous and Unseemly: The Concordia Wells Historical Mysteries by
K.B. Owen

Murder, Honey: The Carol Sabala Mysteries
by Vinnie Hansen

Blogging is Murder: The Jade Blackwell Mysteries
by Gilian Baker

To Kill A Labrador: The Marcia Banks and Buddy Mysteries
by Kassandra Lamb

Steam and Sensibility: The Sensibility Grey Steampunk Mysteries
by Kirsten Weiss

Bound: The Witches of Doyle Mysteries
by Kirsten Weiss

Plus even more great mysteries/thrillers in the *misterio press* bookstore.

Made in the USA
Columbia, SC
11 December 2018